504

MAIGRET AND THE FLEA

GEORGES SIMENON

MAIGRET
AND THE FLEA

TRANSLATED FROM THE FRENCH BY
LYN MOIR

HAMISH HAMILTON
LONDON

First published in Great Britain 1972
by Hamish Hamilton Ltd.
90 Great Russell Street London WC1

Copyright © 1971 by Georges Simenon
Translation copyright © 1972 by Georges Simenon

First published in France 1971
under the title Maigret et l'Indicateur

SBN 241 02262 2

Printed in Great Britain by
Northumberland Press Ltd., Gateshead

When the telephone rang and Maigret groaned with displeasure, he had not the slightest idea what time it could be. He didn't think of looking at the alarm clock. He was coming out of a deep sleep and still felt a weight on his chest.

Barefoot, walking like a sleepwalker, he went to the telephone.

'Hello . . .'

He did not notice that it was not he but his wife who had turned on one of the bedside lamps.

'Is that you, chief?'

He did not recognize the voice straight away.

'Lucas here. I'm on night duty. I've just had a call from the 18th *arrondissement*.'

'Well?'

'They've found the body of a murdered man on the pavement in the Avenue Junot.'

It was right at the top of the Butte Montmartre, not far from the Place du Tertre.

'I'm calling you because of the identity of the dead man. It's Maurice Marcia, the proprietor of the Sardine.'

A truly Parisian restaurant in the Rue Fontaine.

'What was he doing in the Avenue Junot?'

'He doesn't seem to have been killed there. They got

the initial impression that he had been put there after he was already dead.'

'I'm on my way.'

'Do you want me to send you a car?'

'Yes.'

Madame Maigret, still in bed, was still looking at him, but now she got up and poked around with her feet to find her slippers.

'I'll make you a cup of coffee.'

It had been a bad evening, or rather, too good an evening. It was the Maigrets' turn to have the Pardons round. There was an unspoken agreement between them, consolidated over the years.

Once a month Doctor Pardon and his wife had the Maigrets to dinner in their flat in the Boulevard Voltaire. Two weeks later it would be their turn to come to dinner in the Boulevard Richard-Lenoir.

The women would take advantage of the occasion to put out a great spread and to exchange recipes, while the men would gossip lazily, drinking sloe gin from Alsace or raspberry brandy.

The dinner had been particularly successful. Madame Maigret had made a guinea-fowl pie and the superintendent had brought out of his cellar one of the last bottles of an old Chateauneuf du Pape he had once bought a case of, marked down, when he was in the Rue Drouot.

The wine was exceptionally good, and the two men hadn't left a drop. How many liqueur glasses of sloe gin had they had afterwards? At any rate, suddenly awakened at two o'clock in the morning, Maigret did not feel himself.

2

He certainly knew Maurice Marcia. Everyone in Paris knew him. When he was only a detective he had had the man, not at that time a respectable character, in his office for questioning.

Later on, he and Madame Maigret had sometimes dined in the Rue Fontaine, where the cooking was first class.

She brought him his cup of coffee when he was almost dressed.

'Is it important?'

'There's likely to be a scandal.'

'Someone well-known?'

'Monsieur Maurice, that's what everyone calls him. His real name is Maurice Marcia.'

'Of the Sardine?'

He nodded.

'He's been murdered?'

'Apparently. I'd better go and have a look.'

He sipped his coffee and filled his pipe. Then he opened the window a little to see what the weather was like. It was still raining, such a fine rain and so slow that it was invisible except in the haloes of the street lights.

'Are you taking your raincoat?'

'It's not worth it. It's too warm.'

It was only May, a May which had been superb. A storm had appeared to upset the weather and this mist, which had lasted for twenty-four hours now, still remained from it.

'I'll see you when you get back.'

'You know, your guinea-fowl were marvellous.'

'Not too heavy?'

3

He decided not to answer that question, since he could still feel them sitting on his stomach.

A small black car was waiting at the door for him.

'Avenue Junot.'

'What number?'

'You'll probably see a crowd hanging around.'

The streets were as black and shiny as if they had been lacquered. There was almost no traffic. It took them only a few minutes to get to Montmartre, but not the Montmartre of night clubs and tourists. The Avenue Junot was on the edge of the hive of activity and was mostly lined by villas which artists who had begun on the Butte and had remained faithful to it had had built there after they had made their mark.

They saw a crowd on the right-hand pavement and, in spite of the hour, there were lights in the windows and people in their nightclothes leaning out.

The local superintendent had already arrived, a small, thin, shy man who rushed towards Maigret.

'I'm glad you're here, Divisional Superintendent. It's a case which is bound to cause a scandal.'

'Are you sure of his identity?'

'Here is his wallet.'

He held out a black crocodile wallet which contained only an identity card, a driving licence and a note pad with some telephone numbers written on it.

'No money?'

'A whole bundle of notes, three or four thousand francs —I haven't counted them—in his hip pocket.'

'No weapon?'

'A Smith and Wesson which hasn't been used recently.'

4

Maigret went over to the body and it seemed strange to him to be looking down on Monsieur Maurice like that. He was wearing a dinner jacket, as he did every evening, a large bloodstain spread across over his shirt front.

'No traces of blood on the pavement?'

'No.'

'Who found the body?'

'I did,' said a soft voice behind him.

It was an old man whose white hair formed a halo around his head. Maigret thought he recognized a quite well-known painter, but he couldn't remember his name.

'I live in the villa just across the way. I often wake up at night and find it difficult to go back to sleep.'

He was wearing pyjamas over which he had slipped an old raincoat. He had red slippers on.

'When that happens I go to the window and look out. The Avenue Junot is quiet and deserted. Practically no cars go along it. I was surprised to see a black and white shape on the pavement and I came down to see what it was. I rang the police station. These men appeared in a car with its siren blaring and the windows filled up with people trying to see what was going on.'

There were about twenty people, passers-by and neighbours in their nightclothes, looking at the body and the little group of officials. A local doctor said:

'There's nothing more for me to do here. I can assure you he's quite dead. The rest is the forensic surgeon's affair.'

'I have rung him,' the local superintendent said. 'And I have told the Public Prosecutor's Office.'

5

And in fact a deputy public prosecutor was getting out of a car, accompanied by his clerk. He was surprised to find Maigret on the spot.

'Do you think it's an important case?'

'I'm afraid so. Did you know Maurice Marcia?'

'No.'

'You've never had dinner at the Sardine?'

'No.'

He had to explain to him that one was as likely to find people from high society and the arts there as top-level criminals.

Doctor Bourdet, the forensic surgeon who had replaced Doctor Paul, got out of a taxi grumbling, abstractedly shook hands all round and said to Maigret:

'Hah! You're here too!'

He leaned over the body and examined the wound with the aid of an electric torch which he had in his bag.

'Just one bullet, if I'm not mistaken, but large calibre and fired at point-blank range.'

'At what time do you think he died?'

'If he was brought here straight away, the crime must have been committed about midnight. Let's say between midnight and one o'clock. I'll tell you more after the autopsy.'

Maigret went over to Véliard, an inspector of the 18th *arrondissement* who was keeping modestly in the background.

'Did you know Monsieur Maurice?'

'By reputation and by sight.'

'Did he live in the district?'

6

'I'm almost certain he lived in the 9th *arrondissement*. Round about the Rue Ballu.'

'He didn't have a mistress around here?'

It was odd, in fact, for someone with a body on their hands to come to another district and put it down in the peaceful Avenue Junot.

'I think I would have heard about it. Someone who must know is Inspector Louis of the 9th *arrondissement*, who knows the area around Pigalle like the back of his hand.'

Maigret shook hands all round and got into the little black car just as a reporter arrived, a tall redhead, his hair standing on end.

'Monsieur Maigret . . .'

'Not now. Ask the inspector or the local superintendent.'

And he said to his driver, 'Rue Ballu.'

He had kept the dead man's identity card as a matter of habit and he added, after consulting it:

'21 bis.'

It was a rather large private house, like several others in the street, and it had been turned into flats. Among other brass plates on the right of the door was one with the name of a dentist and the note '2nd floor'. On the third floor was a neurologist.

The bell woke the concierge.

'Monsieur Maurice Marcia, please.'

'Monsieur Maurice is never in at this time. Not before four in the morning.'

'What about Madame Marcia?'

'I think she's back. I don't think she'll see you. Try

7

anyway, if you think it's worth your while. First floor, the door on the left. They have the whole floor, but the door on the right is blocked up.'

The staircase was wide, covered in a thick carpet. The walls were of yellowish marble. There was no name on the door at the left, and Maigret rang the bell.

At first there was silence. Then he rang again and at last he heard footsteps inside. Through the door a woman's voice, thick with sleep, asked:

'Who is it?'

'Superintendent Maigret.'

'My husband isn't here. Go to the restaurant in the Rue Fontaine.'

'Your husband isn't there either.'

'Have you been there?'

'No. But I know he isn't there.'

'Just a moment while I put something on.'

When she opened the door she was wearing a golden-yellow peignoir over a white silk nightdress. She was young, much younger than her husband, who was a few years older than Maigret, round about sixty or sixty-two.

She looked at him indifferently, hardly even curious.

'Why do you want my husband at this hour of the night?'

She was tall, very blonde, with the slim supple body of a model or a chorus girl. She could only be thirty at the most.

'Come in.'

She opened the door of a big drawing-room, where she put on the light.

'When did you last see your husband?'

'At about eight o'clock, like any other day, when he left for the Rue Fontaine.'

'Did he go by car?'

'Of course not. It's only five hundred metres away.'

'Does he never take the car to go there?'

'Only when it's pouring.'

'Do you go with him?'

'No.'

'Why not?'

'Because it's not my place. What would I do there?'

'So you spend all your evenings here?'

She seemed surprised by these questions but did not take exception to them. Nor did she show much curiosity.

'Almost all. I go to the pictures sometimes, like everybody else.'

'You don't pop in and say hello to him in passing?'

'No.'

'Did you go to the cinema this evening?'

'No.'

'Did you go out?'

'No. Only to walk the dog. Since it was raining I only stayed outside a few moments.'

'At what time?'

'About eleven? Perhaps a little later.'

'You didn't meet anyone you knew?'

'No. What is the reason for all these questions and why are you interested in what I was doing this evening?'

'Your husband is dead.'

She stared at him. Her eyes were a pale blue, quite expressive. At the same time she opened her mouth as if to cry out but her throat became constricted and she put her hand to her breast. She fumbled for a handkerchief in the pocket of her peignoir and hid her face in it.

Maigret waited, motionless, seated in an uncomfortable Louis XV chair.

'Was it his heart?' she asked at last, crumpling the handkerchief into a ball.

'What do you mean?'

'He didn't like anyone to talk about it, but he had a heart ailment and he was seeing Professor Jardin.'

'He didn't die of heart failure. He was murdered.'

'Where?'

'I don't know. His body was taken afterwards to the Avenue Junot and dumped on the pavement.'

'It's not possible. He didn't have any enemies.'

'Considering he was murdered, he must have had at least one.'

She stood up in one movement.

'Where is he just now?'

'At the Forensic Institute.'

'Do you mean they're going to ...'

'To perform an autopsy, yes. It is inevitable.'

A little white dog came slowly along the corridor and rubbed itself against its mistress's legs. She seemed not to notice it.

'What have they to say about it at the restaurant?'

'I haven't been there yet. What could they say?'

'They could say why he left the Sardine so early. He's always the last one there, and it's he who locks up before counting the takings.'

'Have you worked there?'

10

'No. It's a restaurant pure and simple. There are no song or dance numbers.'

'You were a dancer?'

'Yes.'

'You don't dance any more?'

'Not since I got married.'

'How long have you been married?'

'Four years.'

'Where did you meet him?'

'At the Sardine. I was dancing at the Canary. When I didn't finish too late I would sometimes go there and have a bite to eat.'

'And that's how he noticed you?'

'Yes.'

'Were you a hostess too?'

She winced.

'It depends what you mean by that. If a customer invited us, we wouldn't refuse to drink a bottle of champagne with him, but that was all.'

'Did you have a lover?'

'Why do you ask me that?'

'Because I'm trying to find out who could have a grudge against your husband.'

'I didn't have one at the time I met him.'

'Was he a jealous man?'

'Very.'

'What about you?'

'Don't you think, Superintendent, that this questioning is getting a little distasteful, especially when a woman has just learned of her husband's death?'

'Have you a car of your own?'

11

'Maurice gave me an Alfa-Romeo recently.'

'What about him? What kind of car did he have?'

'A Bentley.'

'Did he drive?'

'He had a chauffeur, but he sometimes drove himself.'

'I'm sorry to have been so unpleasant. Unfortunately it's my job.'

He got up, sighing. Silence reigned in the big drawing-room, whose centre was occupied by a sumptuous Chinese carpet.

She led him to the door.

'I may perhaps have other questions to ask you in the next few days. Would you rather that I summoned you to the Quai des Orfèvres or that I came to see you here?'

'Here.'

'Thank you.'

She answered him with a curt good-evening.

His stomach still felt heavy, his head thick.

'Take me to the Sardine, in the Rue Fontaine.'

There were still several impressive cars in front of the restaurant, and a doorman in livery was walking up and down on the pavement. Maigret went in and breathed the cool air, for the room was air-conditioned.

The head waiter, a man he knew well, Raoul Comitat, rushed up to him.

'A table, Monsieur Maigret?'

'No.'

'If you want to see the boss, he isn't here.'

The head waiter was bald and had a sickly-looking face.

'That's odd, isn't it?' Maigret remarked.

'It almost never happens.'

12

The restaurant, which was spacious, had twenty or twenty-five tables. The beams in the ceiling were exposed, the walls panelled in old oak to three-quarters of their height. Everything was heavy, rich, without most of the tastelessness which almost always goes with the rustic style.

It was after three o'clock. There were only about ten people left, mostly actors and variety artists, eating quietly.

'When did Marcia leave?'

'I couldn't say exactly, but it must have been around midnight.'

'That didn't surprise you?'

'Oh, it did! I doubt if it has happened three or four times in twenty years. Besides, you know him. I've served you and your wife several times. He was always in a dinner-jacket, his hands behind his back. He looked as if he never moved, yet he saw everything. You would think he was in the dining-room, and he would already be in the kitchens or in his office.'

'Did he tell you he was going to come back?'

'He just said, "See you shortly."'

'We were near the cloakroom. Yvonne handed him his hat. I reminded him that it was raining and advised him to take his raincoat which was hanging on one of the hooks.

'"It's not worth it. I'm not going far."'

'Did he seem preoccupied?'

'His expression was difficult to read.'

'Was he angry?'

'Certainly not.'

13

'He hadn't had a phone call just before going out?'

'You'll have to ask at the desk. All the phone calls are taken by the cashier. But tell me, why these questions?'

'Because he was shot dead and his body has been found lying on a pavement in the Avenue Junot.'

The head-waiter's features stiffened and his lower lip began to tremble slightly.

'It's not possible,' he murmured to himself. 'Who could have done that? I can't think of even one enemy. He was basically a good man, very happy, very proud of his success. Was there a fight?'

'No. He was killed somewhere else and then taken to the Avenue Junot, probably in a car. You did tell me he was wearing a hat when he went out?'

'Yes.'

There had been no hat on the ground in the Avenue Junot.

'I have some questions to ask the cashier.'

The head-waiter rushed to a table where the customers were asking for their bill. It was ready and he put it on a plate, half covered with a napkin.

The cashier was a small dark girl, very thin, with lovely dark eyes.

'I am Superintendent Maigret.'

'I know.'

'There's no point in hiding it from you any longer. Your boss has just been murdered.'

'So that's why you looked as if you were hatching a plot with Raoul. I ... I'm flabbergasted. He was standing just where you are not long ago.'

'Had he had any phone calls?'

14

'Just one, a few minutes before he went out.'

'From a man? A woman?'

'That's just what I wondered. It could have been one or the other, a man with a slightly high voice or a woman with a rather deep voice.'

'Had you heard that voice before?'

'No. They asked to speak to Monsieur Maurice.'

'Is that what they called him?'

'Yes. Like all his friends. I asked who was speaking, and he answered:

' "He'll know well enough."

'When I lifted my head, Monsieur Maurice was standing in front of me.

' "Is that for me? What name did they say?"

' "No name."

'He frowned and held out his hand for the phone.

' "Who's speaking, please?"

'Of course, I couldn't hear what the person at the other end was saying.

' "What's that? I can't hear you very well ... What? ... Are you sure? ... If I ever catch you ..."

'The person must have been ringing from a call box because they put more money in. I recognized the sound.

' "I know where that is as well as you do."

'He hung up suddenly. He was on his way to the door when he turned round and went to his office, behind the kitchens.'

'Does he often go there?'

'Rarely during the evening. When he comes in he goes in there to look through the mail. In the evenings, after we close, I take him the money and we check it together.'

'Does the money stay here until the next day?'

'No. He takes it away in a briefcase which is only used for that purpose.'

'I suppose he carries a gun?'

'He takes his gun out of the drawer and puts it in his pocket.'

That night Monsieur Maurice had not been carrying the takings and yet he had gone back to his office for his gun.

'Is there another gun which remains here?'

'No. As far as I know, he only has the one.'

'Would you show me his office?'

'Just a moment ...'

She held out a note to Raoul Comitat.

'This way.'

They went along a corridor with green-painted walls. On the left, a glass panel gave a view into the kitchen, where four men appeared to be tidying up.

'Here it is. I suppose you have the right to go in ...'

The office was simple, without any ostentation. Three good leather armchairs, an Empire desk in mahogany, a safe behind it, and shelves with books and magazines.

'Is there any money in the safe?'

'No. Only the books. We could do without it. It was there when Monsieur Maurice bought the restaurant and he never had it taken away.'

'Where is the gun usually kept?'

'In the right-hand drawer.'

Maigret opened it. There were papers, cigarettes, cigars, but no pistol.

'Does Madame Marcia ring her husband often?'

'Hardly ever.'

'She didn't ring this evening?'

'No. The call would have come through me.'

'What about him. Doesn't he call her?'

'Rarely. I don't remember the last time he did so; it must have been before last Christmas.'

'Thank you.'

Maigret was feeling the weight of his tiredness and he let himself flop on to the back seat of the little black car.

'Boulevard Richard-Lenoir.'

The rain had stopped but the ground was still glistening, and the sky was beginning to grow lighter in the east.

He felt vaguely that there was something amiss in this case. True, Monsieur Maurice was no saint. He had had a fairly stormy youth and had been sentenced several times for procuring.

Then, when he was about thirty, he had moved up in the world, becoming the proprietor of a brothel in the Rue de Hanovre, at that time one of the best-known in Paris.

The brothel wasn't in his name. He spent a good part of his afternoons at the races. When he wasn't there, one was almost sure to find him, along with other villains, playing cards in a *bistrot* in the Rue Victor-Massé.

Some people called him the Judge. They said that whenever a dispute arose among people in the underworld it was he who had the final decision.

He was a good-looking man, dressed by the best tailors, and he wore only silk underwear. He was married and already lived in the Rue Ballu.

17

He had grown plumper with age, which gave him an added dignity.

Oh! Maigret had forgotten to ask the cashier if the man who had phoned had had an accent. That might be important at some time.

For the moment he was at a loss. He remembered something Maurice Marcia had said at one of their last meetings at the Quai des Orfèvres. Marcia was not there on his own account, but because his barman was suspected of having taken part in a hold-up at a branch of one of the big banks at Puteaux.

'What's your opinion of this Freddy?'

The barman was called Freddy Strazzia and he came from Piedmont.

'I think he's a good bartender.'

'Do you think he's honest?'

'Well, Superintendent, it depends on what you mean by that. There's honesty and honesty. When we met, when we were both what you might call beginners at our trades, I didn't consider myself a dishonest man. Which wasn't your opinion, or that of the judges.

'Little by little, I changed. You could say that I've spent forty years of my life becoming an honest man. Well, it's just like it is with converts. They say they are the most devout. So, men who have become honest by their own efforts are more meticulous than others.

'You're asking me if Freddy is honest. I wouldn't stake my life on that, but what I am certain of is that he wouldn't be such a fool as to have anything to do with an affair as badly organized as that.'

The car had stopped in front of his house. He thanked

18

the driver and went upstairs slowly, puffing a little. He could hardly wait to get into bed and close his eyes.

'Are you tired?'

'I've had all I can take.'

Less than ten minutes later he was asleep.

It was almost eleven o'clock when he began to show signs of life, and Madame Maigret hurried to bring him a cup of coffee.

'Goodness!' he exclaimed. 'The sun's shining again.'

'Was it this case in the Rue Fontaine which kept you out last night?'

'How did you know?'

'From the radio. From the papers. They say that Monsieur Maurice was a real Parisian personality.'

'Let's say a character,' he corrected.

'Did you know him?'

'Ever since I started in the Police Judiciaire.'

'Do you know why they dumped his body in the Avenue Junot?'

'I don't understand anything yet. I understand still less why Marcia's gun was still in his pocket.'

'Why?'

'I'm surprised he didn't shoot first. He must have been taken by surprise.'

He sat down in his armchair in his dressing-gown, lifted the telephone receiver and dialled the number of the Police Judiciaire.

At that time Lucas, who had been on night duty, was sound asleep in bed. It was Janvier who answered.

'Not too tired, chief?'

19

'No. I'm all right now. Do you know what's been going on?'

'From the papers and from the reports which have just come in, particularly that from the police station in the 18th *arrondissement*. And I've had a phone call from Doctor Bourdet.'

'What does he say?'

'The shot was fired from about a metre away, perhaps a metre and a half. The gun is probably a short-barrelled revolver, a ·32 or a ·38. He sent the bullet to the lab. As for poor Marcia, his death was almost instantaneous, from an internal haemorrhage.'

'So he didn't bleed very much then?'

'Very little.'

'Did he have a heart defect?'

'Bourdet didn't mention it to me. Do you want me to ring him?'

'I'm going to do that myself. I'll be at the office early this afternoon. If anything new comes up, no matter what, call me.'

A few minutes later he had Doctor Bourdet on the line.

'I suppose you're just getting up,' he said to Maigret. 'I was working until nine o'clock this morning and now they've brought me another customer, a woman this time...'

'Tell me, apart from the wound, did you note anything special, any sign of illness?'

'No. He was a healthy man, very well preserved for his age.'

'Nothing wrong with his heart?'

20

'As far as I could judge, his heart was in good condition.'

'Thank you, Doctor.'

Hadn't Line, Marcia's blonde wife, spoken to him of Professor Jardin, saying that her husband had consulted him from time to time? He rang the professor's house and then the hospital, where he found him.

'I'm sorry to trouble you, Professor. Superintendent Maigret here. I believe one of your patients died a sudden death last night. I mean Maurice Marcia.'

'The restaurant-owner in Montmartre?

'I've only seen him once. I think he was intending to take out a life assurance and before undergoing an official examination he wanted to see a doctor of his own choosing.'

'The result?'

'His heart was perfect ...'

'Thank you.'

'Well,' Madame Maigret asked, 'Was he ill?'

'No.'

'Why did his wife tell you ...'

'I don't know that any more than you do. Would you give me another cup of coffee?'

'What would you like for lunch?'

He could still feel the heaviness he had had in his stomach during the night.

'Some ham, boiled potatoes lightly tossed in oil and a green salad.'

'Is that all? Couldn't you digest the guinea-fowl?'

'I digested them all right, but I think Pardon and I

went a bit heavily on the sloe gin. And that's not counting the wine...'

He got up sighing and lit his first pipe, then stood in front of the open window. He hadn't been there more than ten minutes when the telephone rang.

'Hello, chief. Janvier here. I've just had a visit from Inspector Louis of the 9th *arrondissement*. It was you he wanted to see. He appears to have something interesting to tell you. He's wondering if you could see him at the beginning of the afternoon.'

'Tell him to come to my office at two o'clock.'

With Louis, one never knew. He was a curious man. About forty-five years old, he had been a widower for fifteen years, and always wore black from head to foot, as if he were still in mourning for his wife. And, in his *arrondissement*, his colleagues called him the Widower among themselves.

One never saw him laugh or joke. When he was on desk-duty he worked without stopping. As he didn't smoke, he didn't even have a pipe or a cigarette to light.

Most of the time he worked out of doors, preferably at night. He was probably the one man in Paris who knew the Pigalle district best.

He rarely spoke to a prostitute or a pimp without good reason, and they would watch him go by with some disquiet. He lived alone in the flat which he had once shared with his wife, on the other side of the boulevard, at the bottom of the Rue Lepic. He had even been born in the district. He could often be seen doing his shopping.

He knew the pedigree of all the wide boys of the area, the history of all the girls.

He would go into the bars, never taking his hat off. He would invariably order a quarter-bottle of Vichy. That way he could stay a long time, watching. Sometimes he would speak to the bartender.

'I didn't know Francis was back from Toulon.'

'Are you sure?'

'He's just seen me and slunk off to the gents.'

'I haven't seen him. That surprises me, because he usually comes and talks to me when he comes to Paris.'

'That's probably because of me.'

'Who was he with?'

'Madeleine.'

'That's his old girl-friend.'

He never took notes, and yet all the surnames, the Christian names, the nicknames of all those men and women were filed methodically in his head.

The Rue Fontaine was in his area. He must know more about Monsieur Maurice than Maigret or anyone else. Besides, he wouldn't have come to the Quai des Orfèvres by chance, for he was a shy man.

He knew that he would never get higher than inspector and he was wisely content with that, doing his job as best he could. Having no other passion in life, he devoted himself to it.

'I'm going down to buy some ham.'

He watched her out of the window, walking towards the Rue Servan. He was glad to have a wife like her and there was a little smile of satisfaction on his lips.

How long had Inspector Louis been married before his

23

wife had been run over by a bus? Only a few years at the most, since he had been only thirty at the time. He had been looking out of the window, as Maigret was at that moment, and the accident had happened before his very eyes.

Maigret touched wood, an unusual thing for him to do, and stayed by the window until he saw his wife cross the boulevard again and enter the building.

Louis was the inspector's surname. Maigret had once thought of getting him to join his group, but he was such a lugubrious character that the atmosphere of the inspectors' office would have been affected.

In the office in the 9th *arrondissement*, where there were only three inspectors and a trainee, they fixed it so that Louis worked outside as much as possible.

'Poor man!'

'Are you talking to yourself?'

'What did I say?'

'You said "Poor man". Were you thinking about Marcia?'

'No. I was thinking about a man whose wife died fifteen years ago and who still wears mourning for her.'

'He doesn't wear all black? Nobody does that any more.'

'He does. He doesn't care what people think. Some people, meeting him for the first time, take him for a priest and call him "Father".'

'Aren't you going to shave? Aren't you going to have a bath?'

'Yes. But I feel delightfully lazy.'

He finished his pipe before going into the bathroom.

24

2

The windows in Maigret's office had been opened to the breezes outside and to the noise of cars and buses on the Pont Saint-Michel.

Inspector Louis was sitting on the edge of the chair which the superintendent had indicated to him. He had slow, almost solemn movements, in keeping with his black clothing, which stood out even more on this spring day.

'Thank you for seeing me, Divisional Superintendent.'

His skin was fine and very white, almost a woman's skin, and his thick black moustaches stood out against it. His lips were red, as if they had been made up, and yet there was nothing effeminate about him.

He must have been the timid boy in the class, the one who blushed and stammered as soon as the master spoke to him.

'I would like to ask you something.'

'Go ahead.'

'Will it be the inspectors of the 18th *arrondissement* who investigate the case, since the body was found in the Avenue Junot?'

Maigret had to think before he answered.

'They will certainly question the possible witnesses, check up on a car which stopped in the avenue in the middle of the night, and question the old painter who alerted the police, as well as the other neighbours.'

'But what about the rest?'

'As you know, it's a Criminal Division affair. Which doesn't prevent us from accepting, or even seeking, help from local inspectors. You know Montmartre very well, don't you?'

'I was born there and I still live there.'

'You have come into contact with Maurice Marcia?'

'With him and with his employees.'

He blushed. He was having to make a great effort to say all that he had promised himself he would say.

'Listen, I almost always work at night. I've got to know everybody. In Pigalle they are used to me. I exchange a few words with this man or that. I go into the bars and cabarets where, without waiting for me to order anything, they give me a quarter-bottle of Vichy.'

'I imagine that, since you have come to see me, you have an idea about Marcia's murder.'

'I think I know who killed him.'

Maigret pulled gently on his pipe, a little taken aback, observing the other man with curiosity, even with a certain fascination.

'Are your suspicions based on anything?'

'Yes and no.'

He was embarrassed and didn't dare look the superintendent in the face.

'I had a phone call this morning.'

'An anonymous call?'

'More or less. I've been getting phone calls from the same person for years.'

'A man or a woman?'

'A man. He has always refused to tell me his name.

26

Whenever anything somewhat mysterious happens in Montmartre, he calls me, and he always begins by saying:

' "It's me."

'I recognize his voice. I know he rings from a phone box and he doesn't waste any time, he tells me only the essentials. For example:

' "They're planning an armed robbery in the La Chapelle district. It's Coglia's gang." '

'Coglia has still several years to go in prison,' objected Maigret.

'His old accomplices keep things going.'

'Is your anonymous informer ever wrong?'

'No.'

'Doesn't he ask you for money?'

'No. Nor does he ask me to turn a blind eye on any more or less illegal activities.'

Maigret was growing interested.

'And he rang you this morning?'

'Yes. At eight o'clock, just before I went out to do my shopping. I live alone and I have to do my shopping myself.'

'What exactly did he say to you?'

'Monsieur Maurice was murdered by one of the Mori brothers.'

'Is that all?'

'That's all. Do you know the Mori brothers, Manuel and Jo?'

'We've been trying to catch them red-handed for two years. Up to now we still haven't been able to prove anything against them.'

'I'm watching them too. They don't live together.

27

Manuel, the elder brother, has a comfortable, even luxurious flat in the Square La Bruyère.'

A stone's throw from the Sardine.

'Jo, who is twenty-nine, has a bedroom and a sitting-room in the Hôtel des Iles, in the Avenue Trudaine.

'But you must have all this information in their files. They have a wholesale fruit and vegetable business in the Rue du Caire. One or other of them is there every day. It's a long building which opens straight off the street.'

'Have they any dealings with Monsieur Maurice?'

'They sometimes have dinner at his place. They're not the only villains to go to the Sardine.'

'Did Marcia ever help them?'

'I don't think so. He had grown frightened and held tight to his respectability.'

'Which of the two brothers did your anonymous caller mean?'

'I don't know, but I will certainly be getting another phone call before long. That's why I asked to see you.'

'Do you want to help with the investigation?'

'I would like to assist somehow, officially, in my own way. I have never done anything outside my normal work. You can trust me. I promise to keep you in the picture about anything I find out.'

'Do you know the Mori brothers well?'

'I see them in several bars. Manuel had a very beautiful mistress from Martinique.'

'What has happened to her?'

'She dances and sings in a *boîte* for tourists.'

'Who has he replaced her by?'

'By nobody. I always see him alone or with his brother.

28

He's set up with a girl from the provinces. Her name's Marcelle and she's twenty-two.'

'You don't think she could be the weak link in the chain?'

'She's crazy about Jo Mori and she has a strong character.'

'Do you think she knows what the two brothers are up to?'

'I don't know how far they take her into their confidence. Nor have I ever seen them around with people who could be their accomplices when they pull off a job.'

There had been about ten robberies, all done in the same way, following an identical technique. It was always a château or big estate in the country, within a radius of about a hundred and fifty kilometres from Paris.

The thieves were well-informed. They knew what articles of value, what pictures, what pieces of furniture were to be found in the houses. They also knew if the proprietors were away and how many people would be guarding the buildings.

They operated noiselessly, breaking no windows. In less than an hour, those things which would be easy to sell would be removed. So they had at least one lorry at their disposal.

Now the Mori brothers had two lorries, which they used in their fruit business. As if by chance, it was also two years since they had started up as wholesalers.

Manuel had previously worked for a buyer in Les Halles. Jo had spent three years in an architect's office.

But where were the proceeds of the burglaries stored afterwards? They probably remained near Paris, in a villa or a house rented under another name.

'Who could watch over the stuff?'

'I couldn't swear to it, but I think I know. The Moris'
mother.'

'Do you know her?'

'I've never seen her. I know she exists. She used to
live in Arles with her family. When they came to Paris,
she stayed a few years longer in the Midi with her
daughter. The daughter got married and lives in Marseilles.'

In such a way, over many years, Inspector Louis had
worked alone, patiently, without recourse to the com-
plicated system of the official police force.

'How do you know all that?'

'I watch. I listen. I have contacts in different places,
people whom I can sometimes help ...'

'What became of Madame Mori?'

'She sold up her house in Arles, with all the furniture,
and she hasn't been seen again.'

'I expect you have searched the countryside all around
Paris.'

'I do that on Sundays or on my days off.'

'You haven't found anything?'

'Not yet.'

He blushed again, as if ashamed of his confidence in
himself.

'What do you know about Madame Marcia?'

'You mean the present one? Because there was one
before, with whom he lived for more than twenty years.
They were a very close couple. True, he had picked her
up out of the gutter, but he had turned her into a lady.

30

When she died of cancer, he was very upset, and for several months he was not the same man.'

There had been a time, when he was still young, when Maigret had worked in the streets, then in the stations, the metro, the department stores. At that time he also had known all the shady characters of Paris.

Now he had been shut up in an office, and his chief was shocked whenever he went to interview a suspect at his home or when he ferreted around outside.

'Where did he find his second wife, Line, the one he was living with now?'

'She worked as a dancer at the Tabarin, and more recently at the Canary. I think that's where he met her. In spite of her profession she was a quiet girl, not ostentatiously dressed, and it seems she never went with the customers.

'She's a woman of some education.'

'You're not going to tell me where she comes from, or where her parents live, or how long she stayed at school?'

Inspector Louis blushed once more.

'She was born in Brussels, where her father works in a bank. She went to school until she was eighteen and then went into the same bank. She came to Paris to be with a young man, a painter, who hoped to make his fortune here. He didn't succeed as quickly as he had hoped. Line went into a shop on the Grands Boulevards as a salesgirl.

'Her painter dropped her and she went to the Tabarin where she started by being part of the tableau ...'

Maigret had known the inspector for years. They would

31

meet from time to time, it was true, but they had little contact with each other. For a long time he had considered him a solemn idiot, then had realized that, on the contrary, he was a clever man.

Now he was looking at him almost as if thunderstruck.

'Do you know this much about many people in Montmartre?'

'Well, you know, it mounts up over the years.'

'Do you keep files?'

'No. I have it all in my head. I haven't anything else to do, no other interest in life.'

Maigret got up and opened the door of the inspectors' room.

'Come in here a minute, Janvier.'

And, to the two men:

'I suppose you know each other.'

They shook hands.

'We've just been talking for a long time, Inspector Louis and I, about Marcia's murder. Have you any more on it?'

'Only that a red car stopped for a minute, at about one o'clock, about halfway along the Avenue Junot.'

'Our men are going on with the investigation, of course. But Inspector Louis, who knows several of the people concerned, will work on his own and will keep us up to date with whatever he discovers.

'Do you know the Mori brothers?'

'We suspected them at one time of being at the head of what they call the château gang.'

'Are they still being watched?'

'Not particularly. We only keep track of the places

32

they go. Jo, the younger one, often goes to Cavaillon and the district around there to look for early fruits and vegetables.'

'From today, you're going to put a watch on them day and night.'

'On both of them?'

'On both of them.'

'Still because of the château business?'

'No. This time it's murder. Maurice Marcia's murder.'

Janvier looked mechanically at his colleague from the 9th *arrondissement*. He was obviously not very pleased at Inspector Louis' intrusion into this case.

'Is there anyone else to be watched?'

'The widow.'

'Do you think...?'

'I don't think anything, you know that. I look. We all look.'

He shook Inspector Louis by the hand.

'Are you going back to Montmartre?'

'Yes.'

'Have you a car?'

'No.'

'I'm going there too. Come in mine. I'd like you to come with me, Janvier.'

Janvier took the wheel. Maigret sat beside him smoking his pipe and Louis sat alone in the back seat, rather ill at ease.

He had always dreamed of working directly for the Quai des Orfèvres, and the mission Maigret had given him was like a promotion.

In the Rue Notre-Dame-de-Lorette, Janvier asked,

'Where are we going?'

'Further up. The Rue Ballu.'

'To Maurice Marcia's?'

'Where shall I drop you off?' he asked Louis.

'Anywhere, now that I'm on my home ground.'

'In that case I'll let you off here.'

'You'll know where to find me. My private number's in the book.'

'Thank you for your help.'

Louis got out awkwardly and began to walk along the pavement with regular steps, not hurrying.

Some minutes later Maigret and Janvier rang the doorbell of the former private house. The concierge opened the door. She was hardly forty and was quite pretty. She looked at them through the glass-panelled door which the superintendent pushed open.

'Have they brought the body back?'

'Not yet, but the men from the undertakers are upstairs. I think the body will be here by the end of the afternoon.'

'This is Inspector Janvier who is working on the case too. How long has Madame Marcia lived in this house?'

'Since they've been married. It must be four years.'

'Did they entertain a lot?'

'Hardly at all. As you know, he never came in before three or four in the morning. He would sleep all morning, have his lunch and a siesta, and after that his masseur would come.'

'Did he have dinner here?'

'Very rarely. Most of the time he ate in his restaurant.'

'With his wife?'

'No. I don't think he liked her to go into the Sardine.'

'Why not?'

'I suppose because he was afraid she would meet people he didn't want her to. Don't forget that he was in his sixties and she was barely thirty.'

'What did she do during the day?'

'She would give orders to the cook and the maid. She would sometimes go to Fauchon's or some other luxury shop to buy things you don't find around here. Once or twice a week she went to the hairdresser.'

'In the centre of town?'

'In the Rue Castiglione, I think.'

'And in the evenings?'

'She would read or watch television. Before going to bed she would take her dog out for ten minutes or so.'

'Didn't she ever go to the cinema?'

'Probably she did. Once or twice a week she would stay out all evening.'

'Did she never have company?'

'Never.'

'Thank you. Is she upstairs?'

'Yes. With her dressmaker.'

They did not take the lift, and they rang the doorbell on the first floor. It was a young maid with enormous breasts who opened the door.

'What do you want?'

'To see Madame Marcia.'

'She's busy.'

'We'll wait.'

'Who shall I say?'

'The Police Judiciaire.'

'Just a moment.'

35

She left them in the hall and went towards a door at the end. The drawing-room door was open. The Louis XV furniture had disappeared, as had the big Chinese carpet, and men balanced on ladders were fixing black hangings on the walls.

So they were doing things in the grand manner and the drawing-room was being turned into a mortuary chapel. Obviously the dressmaker was there about the mourning clothes.

'If you will follow me ...'

She showed them into a study or library where there were books from floor to ceiling. They were leather-bound volumes which Monsieur Maurice had certainly never read.

The chairs were comfortable. There was a little bar which undoubtedly held a refrigerator and the desk, which had fittings of red leather, had nothing on it.

In that room the English style had been adopted. A humidor in mahogany inlaid with ivory must have contained expensive Havana cigars. Had these furnishings and things been there when Line first came into the house? Or was it she who had given a certain style to the flat?

'It's a study in which nobody worked very often,' Maigret murmured to Janvier. 'If you had seen the furniture in the drawing-room, you would have thought you were in a museum.'

'It'll make a fantastic mortuary chapel.'

Footsteps approached and they were silent.

She was wearing a black matt silk dress, very simple, and on her finger was a diamond which she probably never took off. She stopped for a moment, framed in the

36

doorway, and there was a look of surprise on her face. She looked from Maigret to Janvier. Was she surprised at confronting two men instead of one? What importance did she give to that? Did it give a more official character to the interview in her eyes?

'This is Inspector Janvier, who is one of my chief assistants.'

She gave a faint nod.

'You must realize I am very busy.'

'We are too, believe me, and we have not come to take up your time for our own pleasure.'

They were all three standing. Since she did nothing about it, Maigret suggested that they sit down.

'Are you going to keep me for long?'

'I don't think so.'

'You could have asked me all the questions you wanted to ask me yesterday. I answered you truthfully. The body will be here at seven this evening.'

The superintendent appeared not to have heard her. Looking around him with an appreciative air, he asked:

'Was the furniture in the flat already here when you came, four years ago?'

'Five,' she corrected him. 'We had been married almost five years.'

'The furniture?'

'It was bought at that time. Before that it was different.'

'Less luxurious, I suppose.'

'Of another style altogether.'

'Which of you suggested changing everything?'

'My husband. He didn't want to see me living in the

37

surroundings which had for so long been those of his first wife.'

'I shan't ask you if they are genuine. I admired the furniture in the drawing-room yesterday.'

'They are,' she answered ungraciously.

'Did you go to buy them with him?'

'He preferred to visit the antique dealers alone and surprise me. But I don't see how this matter of furniture...'

'It has probably nothing to do with your husband's death, but we know from experience that in a case of murder one must neglect nothing. Was your husband very rich?'

'I did not discuss money with him. I only know that his restaurant was doing well and that he took a great deal of trouble to see that it should continue to do so.'

'He was very much in love with you.'

'What makes you think that?'

'One doesn't decorate a flat in such a fashion as this for a woman to whom one is indifferent.'

'He loved me.'

'I imagine that the marriage took place under the communal property law.'

'That's normal, isn't it?'

'When will the funeral service be?'

'Day after tomorrow, in the church of Notre Dame de Lorette. After the ceremony the body will be taken to Bandol, where we have a villa, and buried in the cemetery there.'

'Will you go to Bandol?'

'Of course.'

38

'Will other friends go there?'

'No. I don't know. That has nothing to do with me.'

'Another matter—what is going to happen to the restaurant?'

'It will stay open. Except for the day after tomorrow, the day of the funeral.'

'Who will run it after that?'

She hesitated for a moment.

'I will,' she said, finally.

'Do you think you have sufficient experience?'

'The staff has worked so long with my husband that the business could run itself.'

'Your way of life will be completely changed.'

Maigret knew that she was exasperated by all these questions which seemed to be leading nowhere, but he went on, assuming a heavy manner.

'My way of life is of no concern to anyone as long as I don't break any laws, is that not so?'

'It was just a passing thought. Here you lived almost the life of a recluse. You spent all your evenings alone.'

'No one stopped me from going out.'

'I know. You went to the cinema sometimes. But you had no friends, men or women ...'

The maid entered hesitatingly.

'These gentlemen are asking if we have any green plants, because the place looks empty.'

'Show them the ones on the terrace.'

And, to Maigret:

'You see, I am needed. Your insistence comes as a disagreeable surprise to me, particularly since you were a friend of my husband's, as you led me to believe yesterday.'

'I shall try to disturb you as few times as possible.'

'I warn you that I have decided not to receive you again.'

'I'm sorry about that, because that will oblige me to summon you to the Quai des Orfèvres. Your husband came there often in the past, before he became the proprietor of the Sardine. He didn't have a villa at Bandol either.'

'Do you have to remind me of these disagreeable things?'

'No. Unlike you, he had good friends. I was wondering if you know some of them. Perhaps he had them to stay, in the summer, at his villa in Bandol. The Mori brothers, for example ...'

If she trembled, it was so slightly that he could not be sure.

'Should I know them?'

'That's what I'm asking you. There are two of them, Manuel and Jo. They have a wholesale business in the Rue du Caire.'

'I don't know either of them.'

'They often had dinner at the Sardine.'

'Where I never set foot.'

'One last question. This flat is extremely large. Are you going to go on living here alone?'

'My husband always asked me to, as well as wishing me to keep the restaurant and the house in Bandol.

'"It'll be as if there were still a part of me there," he would say.'

'Was he expecting what happened to him?'

'Certainly not.'

'But he carried a gun in his pocket.'

'Only when he was bringing the money home. Everyone who has to carry large sums of money regularly carries a gun.'

'By the way, once he got home, where did he put the money?'

'In the safe.'

'Where is it?'

'Behind that Delacroix painting which you see to the right of the fireplace.'

'Do you know the combination?'

'No. I'll have to call in a specialist, probably from the firm which makes these safes.'

'Thank you.'

She stood up and he could feel that she was still tense. He felt that she was going over all the questions the superintendent had asked her.

What did they lead to, in fact? Maigret himself would have had difficulty in telling her. He still felt something was wrong. There were some features of this case which he did not like.

He went outside again with Janvier, and the sun was still high and hot.

'Do you think she knows more than she's saying, chief?'

'I'd stake my life on that.'

'Do you mean she could be ... shall we say an accessory?'

'I won't go as far as that, but the story is certainly less clear than she would have us believe.'

'Where are we going?'

'To the Rue Fontaine.'

41

There were no customers at that time, but two of the waiters were setting the tables for dinner. Freddy, the bartender, was wiping bottles and setting them out on the counter.

It was towards him that the superintendent went.

'Isn't Comitat here?'

'He's having a rest in the boss's office.'

'Already?'

'What do you mean?'

'That Monsieur Maurice isn't yet buried and he's already making himself comfortable.'

'You're making a mistake. Even in Monsieur Maurice's time Raoul used always to spend an hour taking a nap in one of the armchairs in the study.'

'Did you know the funeral service will be the day after tomorrow?'

'I hadn't been told that yet.'

'The restaurant will be closed so that all the staff can go.'

'That's the usual thing, isn't it?'

'After that, the body will be buried in Bandol.'

'That doesn't surprise me. The boss was born between Marseilles and Toulon, I don't remember in what village, and he closed the restaurant for a month every year so that he could go to his villa in Bandol.'

'Don't you wonder what's going to become of the restaurant?'

'It's all the same to me. There'll be someone to run it. It's a real gold-mine.'

'Well, from now on your boss isn't going to be a man but a woman.'

'You're joking.'

'Madame Marcia has decided to take her husband's place.'

Freddy made a face, then muttered:

'It's her business, after all.'

'Do you know her?'

'I knew her when she was at the Tabarin. I worked there for two years before I came here. She was in the chorus there.'

'And what do you think of her?'

'I haven't had much occasion to speak to her. When she came to the bar she would ask for her drink, and that was all. I thought she was a bit snooty. Here in Montmartre we're more used to the friendly type. Still, she had class with it. She didn't come from nowhere, and I wouldn't be surprised if she had had a good education.'

'Do the Mori brothers still have dinner here often?'

Freddy saw no harm in the question.

'From time to time. Not regularly. They have to get up early because of their business, you know.'

'Were they still friendly with the boss?'

'Monsieur Maurice would sit down for a few minutes at their table, as he would with good customers. And he would sometimes give them an old brandy from his private store.'

'But Madame Marcia never came?'

'Never.'

'You don't know why?'

'I suppose because Monsieur Maurice was jealous. She's a pretty girl, if you like that type. There was more than thirty years' difference in their ages.'

He looked towards the end of the room.

'Here's Raoul taking up his post.'

The head-waiter had seen them and came up to them, holding out his hand to Maigret and then to Janvier.

'Did you come to see me?'

'We hoped to see you, but our visit wasn't for any particular reason. I was saying to Freddy that the funeral would be the day after tomorrow at the church of Notre-Dame de Lorette.'

'Then we'll close. It would have been more correct for someone to have told me sooner. After all, the whole weight of the business rests on me for the moment. I've been here for sixteen years and she ...'

He stopped, embarrassed. He had obviously been going to say:

'And she has only been sleeping in his bed for five years.'

'Do you know who is going to replace Monsieur Maurice?'

'From the way you ask that question, I can guess. Besides, I already thought about it yesterday. She is, isn't she?'

'Yes. Do you know her?'

'I saw her at Bandol. The boss knew I was on the coast during the vacation and he invited me to dinner at his villa.

'It would be a good place to end one's days, I can assure you. It's not very big. Nothing flashy. Real solid stuff. I'm from the Midi too. With old Provençal furniture I know what I'm talking about. I have rarely seen pieces like Monsieur Maurice's.'

He turned to Freddy.

44

'Haven't you offered these gentlemen anything yet? What will you have?'

'A beer.'

'Me too,' said Janvier, slightly embarrassed.

And Comitat sighed.

'Still, it'll be funny to have a woman for a boss. It'll be a bit like a brothel, won't it!'

'Some of the customers will no doubt feel at home.'

'All kinds of people come here, you know. Ministers of state, theatre people, producers and even bankers. Lawyers too, and doctors, and, as you have just said, some former criminals.'

'Do the Mori brothers still come?'

There was a short silence.

'From time to time. As far as I'm concerned, I've never liked them very much, particularly Manuel. That boy's a real show-off. He has fantastic cars and to look at him you'd think he was as rich as Croesus. Well, it's Jo, his brother, who runs the business. Manuel hardly sets foot in the Rue du Caire and he spends most of his time swanning around Deauville, Le Touquet and places like that.'

'With women?'

'He must have plenty of them, for he's a good-looking boy, but I don't know that he has any serious attachment. It's none of my business. The boss seemed to have a soft spot for him.'

'One thing surprises me. Monsieur Maurice seemed to be very much in love and very jealous of his wife. He would leave her alone at home with the cook and the maid. Now, if I've understood correctly what the cashier

45

said to me yesterday, he didn't take the trouble to phone her, not even to say goodnight.'

'What would you know about that?'

'What do you mean? Was the cashier lying?'

'She wasn't lying, but she doesn't know any more about it than I do. The boss would often go to his office after asking for an open line to be put through to his phone. So he could ring whoever he wanted to.'

'Did that happen often?'

'Once or twice an evening.'

'Do you think he was ringing his wife?'

'He would perhaps deal with other business, but he must have phoned her too.'

'And if she hadn't been there?'

The head-waiter looked at him without answering.

'One must believe that that never happened,' he murmured a moment later.

And one could guess what he was thinking.

The cashier had taken up her post behind the little counter which was reserved for her and she was getting the cash ready.

'May I have a word with her?'

'Of course, superintendent.'

And, as Maigret wanted to pay for the two beers, Comitat added:

'It's on the house.'

'Good evening, mademoiselle.'

'Good evening, superintendent.'

'You told me yesterday, or rather this morning, that Monsieur Maurice asked you to make very few phone calls for him.'

'That's right.'

'And yet he phoned his wife almost every evening.'

'I don't know anything about that. He would some-times ask me to put his phone through to an outside line. In that case I couldn't know whom he was ringing.'

'Was it always at the same time?'

'Never before eleven o'clock. Usually about half-past twelve.'

'Did he make any out of town calls?'

'From time to time. I know that from the telephone statements, since it's my job to pay the accounts.'

'Did he always ring the same place?'

'No. The one which came up most often was a little village which I could hardly find on the map: Les Eglandes, in the Oise.'

'Did you know that your new boss is going to be a woman instead of a man?'

'I thought as much.'

'How will that affect you?'

'It's never very pleasant ... Well, we'll see.'

There were now two customers at the bar. Maigret and Janvier got into the car.

'To the Quai, chief?'

'I'm wondering if I shouldn't go home. I think I'm growing lazy. And it's exhausting to ask questions without knowing where they're leading.'

'Do you think Marcia's murder was premeditated?'

'No. Or else it's one of the most extraordinary crimes I've ever come across.'

'You keep talking about the Mori brothers.'

'Because I've had my eye on them for a long time. It

47

wasn't for nothing that I mentioned the furniture just now, to Madame Marcia's great surprise.

'Maurice was a rough diamond, with no artistic education. Then, more or less day after day, he fills his flat with genuine antiques which are practically museum pieces.'

'The château gang?'

'Why not? There's no lack of taste, at least as far as I know. I intend to have the flat gone over by an expert. If the furniture and furnishings were brought from antique dealers, there will be receipts somewhere.'

'Do you think Line Marcia knows about it?'

'I wouldn't swear she did, on the other hand I wouldn't swear she didn't, either. She took a great deal of trouble to tell us that she had never gone with her husband when he bought the things ...'

It was a traffic-jam, and it took them almost three-quarters of an hour to get to the Boulevard Richard Lenoir.

'See you tomorrow, Janvier.'

'See you tomorrow, chief.'

Maigret wiped his brow before starting up the stairs. He was drenched in sweat.

'Someone rang three times but wouldn't give me a number for you to ring back. He'll try to get you again later.'

'A man's voice? A woman's?'

'It could have been either. He or she kept saying that it was extremely important, a matter of life or death.'

Just when Maigret, exhausted at last, was going to sit down for dinner in front of the open window ...

It was not until about nine o'clock that the sound of the telephone echoed through the flat and Maigret rushed to it, turning off the television as he went.

'Hello. Is that Superintendent Maigret?'

He was hearing the famous voice at last.

'You don't know me, but I know you. I saw you again this afternoon when you visited Line Marcia, and then when you went to the Sardine.'

He had been told of a voice which could have been a man's or a woman's. As far as Maigret was concerned it was more that of a boy whose voice was breaking, and an expression which didn't mean anything came into his mind—a nut-cracker voice. It continually shot from bass to treble and treble to bass.

'Who are you?'

'My name wouldn't mean anything to you. Inspector Louis doesn't know who I am either, and yet I've been ringing him fairly frequently for years.

'I tried to get hold of him today but he isn't at home or in his office. So I decided to speak directly to you. Tell me, when are you going to arrest him?'

'Who?'

'You know as well as I do. Mori. Manuel Mori, for it's the eldest one it's all about.'

Maigret heard the noise of coins being put in. The

unknown man was ringing from a phone box.

'It's urgent, Superintendent. It's a matter of life or death for me. You've put detectives on the tail of the two brothers. I saw them straight away. The Moris are professionals and they'll certainly have seen them too. So they'll know that someone has talked, and *they* know me. They'll certainly think of me.

'I beg you, arrest Manuel at least. He's the most dangerous. He's the one who shot Monsieur Maurice.'

'Why?'

There was suddenly silence at the other end of the line, and Maigret frowned. He waited for a long time, but the phone remained silent.

This time there was no chink of coins, but an emptiness. An agonizing emptiness.

'Did he tell you who he was?' Madame Maigret asked.

'No. He knows a lot and he's in danger.'

He went to bed eventually, tired and worried. He had no way of protecting a man of whom he knew neither the identity nor the appearance.

When he got to the Quai des Orfèvres the following morning it was already hot and he saw Inspector Louis waiting for him on one of the benches in the long corridor.

'Was it me you wanted to see?'

'Yes, Divisional Superintendent.'

'Have you had any news from your kind informer?'

'Yes. He rang me at night. He broke off his conversation with you because he could see through the kiosk window someone he didn't want to be seen by. He also told me that as long as the Mori brothers are at liberty he won't show his face. He's going to run to ground.'

'Do you think he's really in danger?'

'Yes. If not, he wouldn't say he was.'

'What rumours are running about Montmartre?'

'That it was all or nothing for one or other of them, Manuel or Monsieur Maurice. They were both armed. I suppose Mori was the quicker on the draw.'

'And the reason for the crime?'

'When I ask about it here and there, people just smile.'

'Do you think Mori was Line Marcia's lover?'

'That had occurred to me. If it's true, she was chancing not only her luck but probably her life.'

'Have you been along the Rue Ballu this morning?'

'There are already black hangings on the door and many people going in and out.'

'Did you recognize any?'

'It was a mixture. Small shopkeepers, restaurant owners, nightclub girls, pimps ...'

'I'd like to have a look myself.'

He called Janvier and asked him to have a car waiting in the yard.

'Come with me, Monsieur Louis. You know these people better than I do.'

In the Rue Ballu there were little groups gathered on the pavement as if it had been the day of the funeral. The dramatic death of Monsieur Maurice was an event for all Montmartre, and people spoke of it in hushed voices.

'Let's go in.'

They went up to the first floor. Silence reigned in the

51

stairwell. The door of the flat was ajar. From the hall one could smell the scent of candles and chrysanthemums. There were more flowers than there was space to put them and there was no need for greenery to make the vast drawing-room appear less empty.

Line, standing near the door in full mourning, bowed her head to each visitor and shook hands with everyone who held out his hand to her. Her expression was fixed, impenetrable.

When she recognized Maigret her expression was one of annoyance, as if to reproach him for having come and for not respecting the dead.

'My sincere condolences,' he mumbled.

'I'm bearing up as best as I can.'

The coffin was still open and Maurice could be seen, fully dressed, his face peaceful with, it seemed, an ironic smile on his lips. The drawing-room, hung in black with silver teardrops, was lit by a dozen candles whose scent spread through the whole building.

The visitors stopped for a moment to look at the body, dressed as if for some grand ceremony.

'Do you recognize anyone?' whispered Maigret.

'A couple of pimps. The owner of the Sans-Gêne, with his wife who runs the place with him ...'

'Do you think this'll go on all day?'

'Certainly. And tomorrow the Church of Notre Dame de Lorette will be too small to hold everyone.'

They stopped a moment with others on the pavement opposite, watching the visitors go in and come out.

'Here they are.'

A red Jaguar had just stopped at the corner of the

street and two men, still very young, got out. They were both elegant, handsome boys, and there was a kind of defiance in their expression.

Everybody knew them and they knew it. They walked down the middle of the street, bowing discreetly to right and left. When the elder brother saw Maigret he hesitated for a moment and then walked over to him.

'You're giving yourself a lot of trouble, Superintendent, having me and my brother followed. I can save you the expense of these tails by telling you what I'm going to be doing. This afternoon, for example, I'll be in the Rue du Caire with Jo, because we have a big shipment coming in. Tomorrow, after the service, I'll be going to Bandol.

'As for you, Louis, you can go on ferreting about in corners and listening to gossip. Marcia deserved better than that.'

Apparently satisfied with himself, he rejoined his brother and went into the house.

'There's an example for you of the kind of man he is,' murmured Inspector Louis. 'A young wolf with sharp fangs who thinks he's cleverer than anyone else.'

'I'd like to talk to his concierge.'

'She's only on duty in the daytime. At night it's her husband who sleeps on a camp bed in the lodge. He's called Victor and he's well-known in the neighbourhood. He's an inveterate drunk who spends his days going from *bistrot* to *bistrot*.'

'Could you get hold of him?'

'We'll try. We'll have to begin in the Square La Bruyère and the Place Saint-Georges.'

In each of the *bistrots* Inspector Louis drank a strawberry Vichy. As for Maigret, he contented himself with a total of two glasses of beer.

'You haven't seen Victor?'

'He was in here half an hour ago and he must have been just beginning his rounds, because he wasn't drunk yet.'

When the two men caught up with him in the sixth *bistrot* he was beginning to be seriously so.

'Good heavens, Inspector Louis! A quarter bottle of Vichy for the inspector! And you, fat man?'

He was a wreck, the type of man found under the bridges. His shirt was open down his chest and one of his pockets was hanging unsewn.

'I bet you've come to see me. Who's this chap? A doctor?'

'Why would a doctor want to see you?'

'It wouldn't be the first time. They try to shut me up, although I'm the most harmless character in the world.'

That made him laugh.

'It's Superintendent Maigret.'

'I've heard that name before. What does Superintendent Maigret want with me?'

'You sleep in the concierge's lodge at night, don't you?'

'Since my wife was ill and the doctors ordered her to rest.'

'How many tenants are there in the house?'

'Oh, I've never counted them. Let's see, two flats on each floor and an average of three people in each flat. Count it up yourself. It's a long time since I've had anything to do with arithmetic.'

'Do you know Manuel Mori well?'

'I count him as one of my mates.'

'Why?'

'Because from time to time when he comes in he slips me a bottle. It never occurs to the others that I might be thirsty.'

'Does he usually come in late?'

'That depends on what you mean by late. Give me that, Gaston.'

The rough red wine dripped down his unshaven chin. 'Midnight?'

'What about midnight?'

'Did he come in about midnight?'

'Or about five in the morning. It depended on the night. When his girl came to see him ...'

'You mean he brought women in?'

'No, monsieur. Not women. A woman.'

'Always the same one, then.'

'Exactly, always the same one.'

'Tall?'

'Not as tall as him, but taller than I am.'

'Slim? Blonde?'

'And why wouldn't she be slim and blonde?'

'Did she spend the whole night with him?'

'Not at all. You haven't got the idea. She never stayed more than an hour or two.'

'Do you know her name?'

'I'm not a policeman. What about you, do you even know my name?'

'Victor.'

'Victor what? Don't you think I have a surname like

55

everybody else? Well, my name's Macoulet, like my father and my mother, and I was born near Arras. What do you say to that?'

'Was it when he came in with her that he slipped you a bottle?'

'Hey! That hadn't occurred to me. It might well be. That was the case the last time.'

'When was the last time?'

'Yesterday? No. Day before yesterday. I lose the idea of time a bit because all the days and all the nights are the same. It was the night the tenants on the first floor gave a party. The ceiling was shaking over my head and they didn't stop uncorking champagne bottles.'

'What floor does Manuel Mori live on?'

'On the third. It's a beautiful flat, believe you me. He didn't get the furniture in a junk shop or a department store. For example, the bedroom is entirely hung in yellow silk. What do you think of that?'

'Did he come in with her?'

'He always comes in with her. I don't know if he's afraid someone will pinch her from him.'

'Did anyone come in that night, when Mori and his girlfriend were upstairs?'

'Let me think. Funny how thinking gives one a terrible thirst. If you buy me a bottle ...'

Maigret signalled the proprietor in his blue apron to serve him.

'Well, you know, I never see the people who go by. They ring at the front door without ever waking me completely. You mustn't tell that to the building manager, who's a rat. Right. I pull the cord. The people come in and say a name when they go by the glass door. That night the man, because he was on his own, said "Mori". I thought:

'"That's funny. He came in a minute ago with his girl."

'But he might have gone out again to buy a bottle. Or maybe it wasn't him, but his brother. For there are two of them. Did you know there are two of them?

'He pressed the button of the stair-light and he went up.'

'Up the stair or up the lift?'

'I wouldn't know about that. I went back to sleep.'

'You didn't see him go out?'

'Go out, no. The door can be opened from the inside.'

'Did no one make a noise going out?'

'God, yes! The crowd who were at the party on the first floor. They were all stinking drunk, even the women, yapping their way down the stairs.'

'Did you get up and take a look at them?'

'No. I heard the door shut behind them and I didn't pay any more attention.'

'And the girlfriend?'

'What girlfriend? You have one fault, Superintendent. You talk about everyone at the same time. Are you talking about the people on the first floor or about Mori?'

'About Manuel Mori and his mistress.'

'Right. That's clearer already, although you've forgotten the brother.'

'Did he go out again alone?'

'The brother? I don't even know if it was the brother.'

57

'Another beer,' Maigret said. His forehead was covered with sweat. 'All right. Let's say the visitor.'

'I didn't hear him go out.'

'And the floosy?'

'If you knew her, you wouldn't call her a floosy. She's a real lady.'

'The lady, then?'

'She didn't stay up there more than half an hour.'

'Did you see her go out?'

'No. Once again, no. If I had to get up to see people go out it wouldn't be worth having a bed.'

'And after that Mori didn't come down with a heavy bundle?'

'My apologies. Didn't see a thing. No Mori, no bundle. But I heard the car start up.'

'Mori's car?'

'Yes. A little red car, very powerful, which makes a lot of noise when it starts up.'

'What time did he come back after that?'

'I don't know. But when he said his name when he went by I thought they were going too far on the third floor.

'If it hadn't been for the bottle ...'

'There was a second bottle?'

'No. But the first one wasn't rough red like this. It was cognac.'

'Thank you, Victor,' Maigret called after paying the bill.

Once out in the street the superintendent murmured:

'It seems that your informer ...'

'What do you mean, my informer?'

'The one who rings you from time to time to give you tips.'

'I never asked him to. I don't even know him.'

'That's a pity, because he seems to be well-informed. After what I've just heard, I'm beginning to believe that he's afraid. Do you think the Moris are capable of killing him?'

'Or of having him killed. I think they're capable of anything.'

'I wonder if I should get a warrant from the magistrate to have them brought in.'

'Both of them?'

'If the younger brother is as dangerous as Manuel ...'

'What shall I do?'

'You go on picking up information in the neighbour-hood. The atmosphere's right for it. People must be talking among themselves, exchanging information.'

'Will you arrest them today?'

'I'm going to see them in the Rue du Caire first.'

Maigret went, however, to the magistrate's office. He was called Bouteille. He was a man of about fifty who had known Maigret for a long time.

'Have you brought me the murderer already?'

'Not quite. But I'm beginning to have a clearer picture of the case.'

Maigret told what he knew. The two men sat there face to face, smoking their pipes.

When the superintendent had finished, the magistrate growled:

'That's not much in the way of proof.'

'I would like, when I go to see them, to have an order

59

for their arrest in my pocket. And also a search warrant.'

'Made out in the name of both brothers?'

'That would be better. I don't know where the informer's hideout is. It would seem that Jo is as dangerous as Manuel.'

Judge Bouteille turned to his clerk.

'Make out two warrants in the names of the Mori brothers, Manuel and Joseph.'

Maigret gave the address of each one.

The magistrate led him to the door.

'The case is going to create a scandal.'

'It's doing so already.'

'I know. I've read the papers.'

One of them coolly displayed the headline:

WAS MAURICE MARCIA A GANG-LEADER AND WAS HE KILLED BY A RIVAL?

Another made allusion to all the little mysteries around Pigalle and to the role of the police force, which too often kept its eyes closed.

'The investigation looks as if it will be difficult and one wonders if we will ever know the end of the story.

'The funeral service tomorrow promises to attract a considerable crowd, since the proprietor of the Sardine had friends not only in the neighbourhood but all over Paris.

'But they will not all be there.

'As for Superintendent Maigret, he refuses to make any statement. At the present moment it is not even known if he will go to Bandol tomorrow.

'He merely repeats,

' "I am continuing with my investigation." '

It was on the edge of Les Halles, where the buildings had not yet begun to be demolished, but where all activity had ceased and been transferred to Rungis.

The Rue du Caire was one of the many streets where could be found wholesalers and warehouses as well as one-night hotels and shabby *bistrots*.

In a year's time everything would probably be a heap of rubble.

When Maigret got out of his taxi, he saw two detectives walking up and down on the pavement. For a moment he wondered why there were two, then he understood. One was watching Manuel Mori and the other his brother Jo.

'You know they've spotted you, boys?'

'That's why we're not hiding. The elder one walked over to me quite calmly and said, blowing the smoke from his cigarette in my face, just like in the flicks:

' "Don't trouble to play hide-and-seek, copper. I know you're there and I won't try to get away." '

The warehouse was a long empty room, without any frontage at street-level, which was shut at night with a sliding metal grille. In the middle Maigret could see a lorry unloading. One of the men, in a grey overall, was on the lorry, passing down the boxes of fruit to his mate who caught them in mid-air and piled them along the wall.

Jo Mori, a few metres away, his hands in his pockets, a cigarette in his mouth, was watching the unloading with the air of a man thinking of other things. He did not

61

frown when he saw Maigret, did not make as if to move towards him.

In the right-hand corner of the warehouse, near the street, there was a glassed-in office where Manuel, hat on the back of his head, was going through a pile of receipts. He too had undoubtedly seen the superintendent, but he wasn't going to move.

Maigret pushed open the door, took the only empty chair and sat down, then began to fill his pipe.

It was Manuel who weakened first and murmured:

'I was expecting you.'

Maigret still said nothing.

'Besides, I've just telephoned my lawyer. He agrees with me that you talk too much, you and the funereal inspector who has been skulking around Montmartre as long as anyone can remember. You're both asking too many people too many questions.'

Maigret lit his pipe carefully without appearing to pay any attention to the man speaking to him.

'Sometimes insidious questions can do as much damage as accusations, and in that case it's slander.

'As far as my brother and I are concerned, it's all the same to us, but you're implicating other people. As for the Flea, because he has stuck his nose into what doesn't concern him, it could be the end for him.'

And so it was that Maigret, without asking him, finally learned through one of the Mori brothers the identity of the man who had telephoned him the previous evening and who phoned in information to Inspector Louis on a more or less regular basis.

'Where were you the night before last at half-past twelve?'

'At home.'

'No. You had been there half an hour earlier and you weren't alone.'

'I have the right to have any visitors I like.'

'But not to murder people who come to visit you.'

'I haven't murdered anyone.'

'And I'm sure you don't have a gun at all, not even a ·32 revolver.'

'What would I do with one?'

'You found a use for one that night. It's true you could always plead self-defence.'

'I don't have to defend myself against anybody.'

'I'd like to look over your flat.'

'Go and get a warrant from the magistrate.'

Maigret took it out of his pocket and held it out to Manuel, together with the two warrants for arrest.

It was clear that Mori hadn't expected this, and he saw the danger, gave a start and dropped cigarette ash over his waistcoat.

'What does this mean?'

'What these papers usually mean.'

'Are you going to take me in?'

'I don't know yet. Probably. Do you still refuse to let me into your flat?'

He got up for a moment, trying to recapture his arrogance. He opened the door slightly.

'Hey, Jo. Come here a minute.'

His brother had taken off his jacket and rolled back the sleeves of his white shirt.

'You know what these papers mean, don't you? There's one for you, one for me, and another for the two of us, the search warrant. You haven't got a body stashed in your cupboard, have you?'

The younger Mori didn't join in the joking but read through the warrants carefully.

'What then?' he asked.

One couldn't tell if he was speaking to his brother or to Maigret.

'When I've finished with your brother I'll go to your hotel. You wait for me there.'

'Do you have a car?' asked Manuel.

'A taxi.'

'You wouldn't rather I drove you?'

'No. But follow my taxi without trying to pass it.'

Maigret picked up the detective charged with following Manuel.

'Where are we going?'

'To his place in the Square La Bruyère.'

'He's following us.'

'That's just what I asked him to do.'

It was only a stone's throw from the Rue Fontaine. Marcia's flat in the Rue Ballu was a stone's throw from the restaurant. As for Jo, he lived in the Hôtel des Iles in the Avenue Trudaine, only five minutes away.

'The funeral's tomorrow, isn't it?'

'The funeral service is tomorrow, but then the body's being taken to Bandol, where he'll be buried.'

The six-storey building was modern, luxurious.

'What shall I do? Shall I come up with you?'

'I'd rather you stayed downstairs.'

64

The red Jaguar stopped behind the taxi.

'I'll show you the way.'

They went past the lodge, whose curtain moved.

'It's on the third floor.'

'I know.'

'Doesn't it worry you, taking the lift with me?'

'Not at all.'

'You might well be afraid. I'm younger and stronger than you.'

Maigret merely looked at him as one looks at a boasting child.

Manuel took a key out of his pocket, opened the door and ushered in the superintendent in front of him.

'You see, I have no maid. An excellent woman comes in every day to do the cleaning, but as I'm often asleep at this time of day she only comes in the afternoons.'

The drawing-room was not big, particularly in comparison with the one in the Rue Ballu, but it was furnished just as carefully. It led into a dining-room where a still-life by Chardin, showing pheasants in a basket, looked quite authentic to Maigret.

'Chardin?'

'I believe so.'

'Do you like painting?'

'I like it quite a lot. Just because I sell tomatoes and fruit doesn't mean I have no appreciation of the fine arts.'

His tone was bantering. In the bedroom, the bed was unmade. This room was the only modern one, very bright, very gay. It gave on to a bathroom so big that there was a punch-ball set up in the middle.

'End of visit. You've seen everything.'

'Not yet. There's something missing in the bedroom.'

'What?'

'In the middle of the room there used to be a small rug which has left a lighter patch on the carpet.'

Maigret leaned over.

'Besides, you can still see in the pile of this carpet coloured threads which probably come from the missing rug.'

'Look for it.'

'I wouldn't be so stupid. May I?'

He picked up the telephone and asked for the Police Judiciaire, then for the laboratory.

'Is that you, Moers? Maigret here. I want you to come to the Square La Bruyère with two or three men. You'll find one of our detectives at the door. Go up to the third floor. What am I looking for? Anything.'

This time Manuel had lost his arrogance.

'They'll come and turn over everything in the flat.'

'Very likely.'

'I can tell you right now that the rug you're talking about never existed.'

'Then we'll find out what those coloured threads come from.'

'From a girlfriend's coat ...'

'No. Madame Marcia, Line if you prefer, is a woman of taste who wouldn't wear a coat mixing green, red and yellow.'

'My lawyer has the right to be present during the search, I suppose?'

'As far as I'm concerned I don't see anything against it.'

It was Manuel's turn to make a phone call.

'Hello. May I speak to Maître Garcin, please. This is Manuel Mori. It's very urgent.'

He was getting feverish.

'Garcin? Listen, I'm calling you from home. Superintendent Maigret has a search warrant. He has found some threads he doesn't like on the carpet. Just now he called in men from the forensic department. Can you come . . . ?

'What's that? I am obliged to let them go through all the furniture and the drawers? That isn't all. He has a warrant for my brother's arrest and another in my name.

'No. He told me that he doesn't know yet if he'll use them. Listen, if I haven't rung you by, let's say, four this afternoon, do everything you can to get us out again. I have no desire to spend the night in the Mousetrap. Besides, the funeral service is tomorrow, and I was planning to go to Bandol afterwards for the burial.

'Yes, she's all right. Thanks, pal. See you later.'

His conversation with the lawyer had bucked him up a bit.

He was surprised to hear Maigret say to him:

'If you had told me you were going to Bandol . . .'

'What difference would that have made?'

'I wouldn't have worried about the warrants just now. I wasn't thinking of Line, who will probably be needing you.'

'What are you insinuating?'

67

'Only what everyone around Pigalle knows. You don't have two or three girlfriends a week any more.'

'My private life is my own concern.'

'You have the right to sleep with the wife of a friend, that's true, but not to shoot him in the chest.'

The doorbell rang. Moers was accompanied by two men carrying small cases.

'This way. It's in the bedroom. No point in asking you what was on that paler patch ...'

'A rug, of course.'

'There are some threads left on the carpet. I'd like you to gather them up and examine them. In general, the whole flat needs a thorough going-over. I would be interested to find plans of houses or châteaux, for example, or correspondence with antique dealers or art dealers.'

This time Mori was dumbfounded and made no attempt to hide it.

'What's all this about, this new story?'

'It's nothing yet, just an idea, but it might turn into something.

'I'll let you get on with your work, Moers. I have something else to do. I may perhaps need you there too.'

And, turning to Manuel:

'I'll leave you too. Until I order to the contrary, you are at liberty, but you are forbidden to leave the city.'

'What about Bandol?'

'I'll tell you that tomorrow morning.'

'May I ring Line?'

'You've just come from there.'

Manuel shrugged his shoulders.

68

'You've got so far it isn't worth denying it. Particularly since we have done nothing wrong.'

'Congratulations.'

Several minutes later Maigret entered the Hôtel des Iles which, though not a luxury establishment, was comfortable and unusually clean, probably inhabited by permanent residents.

'Jo Mori, please.'

The young lady on the other side of the counter looked at him, smiling.

'Second floor. Number 22, Monsieur Maigret.'

'Did he tell you he was expecting me?'

'No. He told me was expecting someone. But I recognized you as soon as you opened the door.'

Maigret took the lift, knocked at number 22 and the door opened at once. It was Jo, who had left the Rue du Caire so that he would be at home when the superintendent arrived.

'What have you done with my brother?'

'I left him at home. With, it's true, specialists from the forensic laboratory who are going over the place with a fine tooth-comb.'

'You haven't arrested him?'

'Line will be needing him tomorrow. He has to go to Bandol. What about you?'

'I wasn't planning to go. What Line are you talking about?'

'You can drop that. That's all finished with. Your brother has admitted he's her lover.'

'I don't believe you.'

They were in a little pearl-grey drawing-room, which

was somewhat old-fashioned but nonetheless pleasing. Jo, after hesitating, reached out for the phone and dialled his brother's number.

Maigret, his hands behind his back, looked around him, opened a door at random and found himself face to face with a girl wearing only a peignoir which hung half open.

'You're Jo's mistress, I suppose? That's a stupid question, since I find you in his room, near the unmade bed, with some of your clothes on the chair.'

'Is there anything wrong in that?'

'Not at all. How old are you?'

'Twenty-two.'

He heard Jo's voice behind him.

'He's with her already. I didn't have time. What about you? Is it true he's letting you go to Bandol and that you've told him about Line? You might have warned me.

'I don't know. He's talking to her in the bedroom now. You know her. She could talk for hours; unfortunately I've never found a deaf-mute who appeals to me.'

He hung up quickly and appeared at the doorway of the bedroom.

The girl was saying:

'My name's Marcelle. Marcelle Vanier. I'm from Béziers, but I came to Paris as soon as I could.'

'How long have you been with Jo?'

'A month, and I haven't any illusions about it. I don't think I'll last another month.'

'Close your robe,' the young man said dryly.

And, turning to Maigret:

'If you were to tell me exactly what you are looking for, we might get somewhere. You know we have a lorry being unloaded and then I have to deliver the merchandise.'

As if he hadn't heard, the superintendent went on speaking to Marcelle.

'Where were you the night before last?'

'From what time?'

'From eleven o'clock.'

'We went to the pictures, Jo and I. We came back straight after, because he was tired.'

'At what time did the phone ring?'

She opened her mouth, shut it again and looked questioningly at Mori.

'There's no harm in that,' he said. 'It was my brother who was ringing to tell me that he intended to make a trip to the provinces in the next few days.'

'To Bandol?' the superintendent asked slyly.

'To Bandol or somewhere else. He didn't say.'

'If he spoke of Bandol, it was a premonition, since Maurice Marcia wasn't dead then.'

'What would I know about that?'

'It was in all the papers yesterday, with the time of death. About half-past midnight.'

'That's quite possible and it doesn't interest me.'

'Have you any paintings here?'

'What paintings?'

'I don't know. There are a lot of art-lovers in this case.'

'I'm not.'

'And this furniture is good honest hotel furniture.'

'What else would it be?'

'Is this where you keep the receipts and the business papers?'

'In the Rue du Caire, at the office, of course.'

'Are you working, Mademoiselle Marcelle?'

'Not at the moment.'

'What did you do before you met this character?'

'I was a barmaid in a bar in the Rue de Ponthieu. Perhaps I was wrong to leave my job.'

'I'd agree with that.'

'What do you advise me to do?'

'Hey, watch it!' interrupted Jo, his fists clenched.

'Gently, boy, I'm not taking you in today. Take advantage of your freedom for a bit yet. But don't take it into your head to leave Paris.

'Oh, yes! One more bit of advice—don't lay a finger on the Flea, if you should meet him. That could cost you very dearly.'

And Maigret went downstairs, filling his pipe. He had forgotten the girl at the reception desk and he was surprised when a young voice called out to him:

'Goodbye, Monsieur Maigret.'

When he arrived at the Quai des Orfèvres, Maigret called Janvier into his office straight away.

'Anything new on the Marcia case?'

'Only a phone call from Inspector Louis, who would like to speak to you.'

'Is he in his office?'

'No. He'll be in the Restaurant du Rhône, in the Boulevard de Clichy, at half-past twelve.'

'Will you have lunch with me?'

'Certainly. Besides, my wife is at her mother's today and I would have eaten in a restaurant anyway.'

The superintendent rang Madame Maigret.

'I have a lot of work and I won't be home for lunch.'

She had known it in advance. Every time a case got to a certain point he needed in a way to play truant, that is to say, to lunch with his colleagues at the Brasserie Dauphine.

It was a way of keeping his hand in. The two men walked slowly over to the *brasserie* and stood at the counter, where there were already several men from the Quai des Orfèvres.

'I'll have a small *pastis* for a change,' growled Maigret.

That happened rarely. Since his old friend Pardon had warned him, he drank much less than before and he would keep his pipe in his mouth, unlit, for a long time.

'You don't know what Louis wants with me?'

'Well, you know, he puts on that mysterious act.'

'He's an amazing man, but he couldn't join our group. He needs to work alone.'

The proprietor came over to shake hands with them. Little by little, he had grown completely bald and since the process had taken years it had gone unnoticed.

'What is there for lunch?'

'*Andouillettes*. But if you would rather have a steak ...'

'*Andouillettes*,' Maigret cut in.

'For me too,' echoed Janvier.

They went into the dining-room, where there were only four tables occupied, two of them by lawyers. They were in the family, so to speak. Maigret had his corner by the window, from which he could see the Seine and the boats passing. From his office too he could see the boats going by. It had been so for more than thirty years, and he never tired of it.

'When you get back to the Quai, would you be so good as to ring Orly? I want a seat in a plane for Marseilles tomorrow. Preferably in the middle of the day.'

'Are you going to Bandol?'

'Yes. Unofficially, of course, since it's out of our jurisdiction.'

'There's certainly an Air-Inter flight.'

'It's half-past twelve. Would you ring Inspector Louis and ask him to come to my office as soon as he has had lunch?'

By quarter past one the Widower was seated facing the superintendent, and the leaves on the trees rustled on the other side of the open window. Maigret had taken his jacket off. Louis was still in black, even to his tie.

'I had a phone call this morning from the girlfriend of my anonymous caller ...'

Maigret could not hide a smile.

'She didn't tell me her name. She's worried because her friend hasn't given any sign of life for forty-eight hours.'

Maigret waited patiently for him to go on.

'Another rumour, more vague. At least three or four villains have suddenly felt the need to leave Montmartre. And, as if by chance, they are friends of the Mori brothers.'

'I have some news for you too, Inspector. I know who your anonymous caller is.'

Louis' face grew quite red. It seemed impossible to him that the superintendent in twenty-four hours could make an identification which he had not been able to manage over many years.

'Who is it?'

'Do you know the Flea?'

'Everyone in Montmartre knows him.'

'It's him. Manuel Mori told me so himself, either giving himself away or thinking that I knew already.'

For almost thirty years Maigret had known the man, who was called the Flea because he was only four feet eleven. He was also thin, with a strange face in which the mouth took up almost all the space. And that mouth could in an instant take on any conceivable expression, as if it were made of rubber.

He had worked as a messenger boy at the Cellar Rat, a cabaret in the Place Pigalle which was then very elegant, where most of the customers wore dinner jackets. He wore

75

a red uniform with a short jacket and a braided cap, and he stood at the door, ready to take customers' messages anywhere.

The Cellar Rat had disappeared. The Flea, whose real name was Justin Crotton, had worked for several years now in the *brasserie* in the Rue Victor Massé where the underworld gang-bosses hung out.

He was still just as thin, just as agile and as capable of slipping in anywhere, but his face was lined. From a distance he looked like a boy. Close up, he looked fully his age of forty-five or forty-six.

'And to think I didn't recognize his voice,' Louis moaned.

'He must have disguised it as much as possible.'

'Not so much as all that. Now that you've told me, I can see it. I can't forgive myself for not having thought of him.'

'What has he been doing lately?'

'He was living in the Rue Fromentin with a hostess at the Canary in the Rue Pigalle.'

'Her pimp?'

'More or less. I don't know. It's a bit strange for a pretty girl to set up with a runt like that. He was born in Paris, in the Boulevard de la Chapelle, and I needn't tell you what his mother did for a living. She sent him to one of her sisters at Saint Mesmin le Vieux, in the Vendée. He came back to Paris when he was fourteen and managed to get by on his own.'

'He's in danger,' Maigret said gravely.

'Do you think the Moris would dare ...'

'They themselves are out of it. But they have enough

76

killers at their disposal to put down a troublesome witness.'

Inspector Louis couldn't keep off the subject.

'The Flea! And nobody suspected him. He was considered to be an inoffensive creature, not quite a man, a kind of boy with a wrinkled face. He hung around villains who wouldn't worry about talking in front of him.

'I think he dreamed of being one of them. I wouldn't be surprised if they hadn't used him as a lookout from time to time.'

'What's the name of his girlfriend?'

'Blanche Pigoud. 28 Rue Fromentin. A stone's throw from the Boulevard de Clichy, where I've just been having lunch.'

'Do you know her?'

'Only by sight. I've never had anything on her.'

'She must go to bed in the small hours. We're likely to find her at home.'

'Unless it's her day at the hairdresser's. Those girls only get up early to go to the hairdresser.'

Maigret called Janvier.

'Do you want to come with us? We're going to Montmartre again.'

'Shall I take a car?'

'Of course.'

The three of them went off. It was a beautiful day, a litle too warm for May, and it felt thundery.

The Rue Fromentin was quiet. Number 28 was a fairly modern, well-built block of flats.

'Shall we all go up?'

'I'll go up alone at first, so as not to frighten her. No,

wait. It would be better if Inspector Louis came with me, since he's the one she phoned.'

'Second floor, facing the street,' the concierge told them.

Kitchen smells hung around the stairwell and a baby was crying somewhere. Maigret rang the bell. It was a long time before a young, rather plump girl, naked under a light peignoir, opened the door.

She recognized Inspector Louis.

'Have you found him?'

'Not yet, but Superintendent Maigret would like to talk to you.'

'You can see how I am. I was asleep. I haven't even combed my hair.'

'We'll give you time for that,' Maigret said jovially.

The girl had an open expression, even a little naïve. She must have been about twenty-five, and the life she led had not yet taken away all her freshness.

'Come in. Sit down. I'll be with you straight away.'

She went into a bedroom which must have opened into the bathroom.

If the superintendent had not been used to women of the kind scorned by middle-class ladies, he might have been surprised by the décor surrounding them.

The living-room was comfortably furnished. The same so-called modern furniture could be found in half the flats in Paris. It was carefully polished, as was the floor. Besides which, there was a slight smell of disinfectant everywhere.

Pushing open a door, Maigret discovered an immaculate kitchen where not a thing was out of place.

'Would you like a cup of coffee?' asked the girl when she reappeared, still naked under her peignoir, but with

78

her face washed and a light coating of make-up on.

'No, thank you.'

'Do you mind if I have one? In my job, I can't always refuse a drink. When he can, Bob serves me cold tea made to look like whisky, but with some customers that's not possible. If you like, there's beer in the refrigerator. Justin adores beer and he's always hoping it will make him go fat. Did you know he only weighs ninety pounds?

'He was going to be a jockey, but his apprenticeship only lasted two days because he was afraid of the horses.'

'He isn't afraid of the Pigalle toughs.'

She had switched on an electric percolator. The kitchen was fitted out with all the most modern gadgets.

'You didn't say, about the beer.'

'I would like a glass.'

'Your inspector only drinks Vichy, and I don't have any in.'

'How do you know he only drinks Vichy?'

'He comes into the Canary from time to time. He goes into all the *boîtes*. He sits at a corner of the bar and listens. He knows a lot more than he looks as if he knows.'

'Did you know about the Flea's telephone calls?'

'Not exactly.'

She took her coffee into the living-room and Maigret followed her with his glass of beer.

'He's a funny boy. Inspector Louis can tell you that, can't you, Inspector?'

'I've always wondered why you've set up house with him.'

'First of all, because I can't stand most pimps. Really

79

I was born to be a good little middle-class housewife and I'm never as happy as when I'm doing housework.'

They were all sitting in armchairs.

'But in my job one needs a man.'

'Even if he's a little runt like Justin Crotton?'

'Don't you believe that. He is still a child in certain ways, but he has more nous than he lets on.'

She paid no attention to her peignoir, which was hanging wide open. Her skin was very pale, probably very soft.

'His dream has always been to become one of the real villains. To start off, like most of them, he wanted to be a pimp.'

'Is that what he is now?'

'That's what I let him think. That lets him take himself seriously. He still runs errands for people as he did when he was a messenger-boy. From time to time he puts on mysterious airs, even with me, and he just says:

'"Don't be surprised if I don't come for a night or two. We have something big on."'

'Was it true?'

'It was true that something big was being prepared by one gang or another but he wasn't in on it. What I didn't know was that he would phone all the information he had to the inspector. That also made him feel more important in his own eyes.'

'What has been happening these last two days. Has he told you?'

'Not exactly. One morning he came in over-excited.

'"There was a row last night, something which will be on the front page of all the papers, and there'll be a great scandal."

80

' "A robbery?"

' "Worse than that. A murder. And the victim is one of the best-known people in the neighbourhood."

' "Can't you tell me his name?"

' "It'll be in all the papers soon. It's Monsieur Maurice."

' "The proprietor of the Sardine?"

' "Yes. And I'm the only person, apart from the murderer and his mistress, who knows who did it."

' "I'd rather not know who it is." '

She lit another cigarette, for she had already had one lit when she came out of the bathroom.

'I asked him what he was going to do. He answered:

' "Don't worry about me."

' "You're not going to inform on the man, are you?"

' "You know that's not my line."

' "Does he know you know?"

' "If he knew, I wouldn't make old bones." '

She was silent for a moment, blowing the smoke in front of her.

'In a way it was the biggest day of his life.

' "If you knew what it was all about ... One of the biggest bosses of Montmartre ... As for his mistress ..."

' "Don't tell me anything."

' "All right. You'll learn the truth in the papers. If the papers dare to publish it."

'He went out that morning, and I haven't seen him since. Last night at the Canary people were looking at me in a funny way, and two men I don't know never took their eyes off me.

'I stayed at the bar as usual. I was joined by a customer

from the provinces who always comes to see me when he's in Paris. We went to the hotel and when we came out one of the men was walking up and down on the pavement.

'At first I was afraid for the Flea. Everyone calls him that, and now I do too. Besides, he's quite proud of it. It's a kind of recognition. He likes to make faces too, to amuse people.'

'He rang me,' said Inspector Louis in a neutral voice.

'That's what I thought. That explains his mysterious manner, and what he said when he went. Is he really in danger?'

It was Maigret who answered.

'There's no doubt about that. Monsieur Maurice's murderer knows that the Flea has informed on him.'

'What about me? Do you think they will get at me?'

'Are you still being followed?'

'Last night one of the men was still at the Canary. He was called to the telephone and he went away after that, not without giving me a funny look.'

'If I'm not mistaken, they're running to ground all over France.'

'What about the Mori brothers?'

'Who told you about them?'

For there had been no mention of them in the papers or on the rado.

'Everyone around here is talking about them. Have they gone too?'

'No. But we are keeping an eye on them both.'

'Do you think it was them?'

'I can't answer that question. What time do you usually leave the house?'

'I do my shopping at about two or three, because I like to cook. At about ten in the evening I get dressed for work and I go to the Canary. I sit at the bar and I wait. Sometimes I wait for two hours or so, sometimes only a few minutes, and I have been known to wait until closing time.'

'In an hour's time there'll be a plain-clothes policeman in the street. Don't be surprised when he follows you. He'll do everything he can, and more, to protect you.'

'Should I go to the funeral service tomorrow? Everyone's going.'

'Yes, do. I'll be there too. Just like your guardian angel.'

'That makes me think of my catechism.'

The two men stood up.

'If you hear anything, ring the Police Judiciaire. Ask to speak to me or to one of my men in the Criminal Division. Inspector Louis is rarely in his office.'

'Thank you, Superintendent. Goodbye, Inspector ... If you have any news of Justin ...'

'I hope we won't have any. He has recognized the danger and gone into hiding. He doesn't need to go far, for he knows Montmartre inside out and there are places where a lad like him can live for weeks without being seen.'

'Let's hope so,' she said, touching the wooden table.

They found Janvier outside.

'Well?'

'She's afraid, of course, and I can't blame her. Afraid for the Flea and for herself. I promised her that one of our men would be in front of the house in an hour and that she would be followed wherever she went. Don't forget to arrange it when we get back to the Quai. Someone who can go into a fairly elegant *boîte* without being conspicuous.'

Maigret turned back to Louis.

'You stay on watch just now. As soon as our man gets here you'll be free again.'

'Right, Superintendent.'

Once he was at the wheel again, Janvier asked:

'What's she like?'

'Very nice. If things had gone differently for her, probably when she was about seventeen or eighteen, she would have been a marvellous wife and housewife.'

'Did she know anything?'

'About the Flea's phone calls? She only suspected it two days ago. It's extraordinary. That little man with the clown's face has been able to be one of Inspector Louis' informers for years without anyone suspecting. He must have enjoyed the rôle, which gave him self-confidence. When this man or that was arrested he could say to himself:

' "That was my doing!"'

'And it was true!'

During the afternoon Maigret went up to the attics of the Palais de Justice, where Moers' empire was, the forensic laboratory.

Specialists were needed in nine out of ten cases, even if only for fingerprints, and yet there were less than a dozen of them, working in white overalls in the rooms with sloping ceilings.

'I suppose it's too soon to have any news?'

Moers was an unassuming man, thin as a rail, whose suit always needed pressing. He had been at the Quai for so long that it was impossible to imagine Criminal Identity without him. He was always ready for work, whatever the hour of day or night. True, he was a bachelor and there was no one waiting for him in his student's digs in the Latin Quarter.

'One fact is already clear,' he answered in his rather monotonous voice. 'Quite recently, yesterday afternoon probably, all the furniture was polished and all the door-knobs, the ashtrays, even the smallest object, wiped to remove fingerprints.

'The only prints we lifted were those of the tenant, Manuel Mori, whose card I found in Records, and those of the cleaning-woman, who did go to the Square La Bruyère yesterday afternoon, the concierge told me. I forgot the other prints—yours.'

'Not one fingerprint overlooked?'

'Not one. One would almost say professional work.'

'It is professional work. What is the date of the card you found in Records?'

'It's fourteen years old.'

'Theft?'

'Yes, during the holidays, in a private house in the Avenue Hoche.'

'How many years did he get?'

'He was only eighteen, and his case-sheet was clean. Besides, he was considered to be only an accomplice, for the job was carried out by five men.'

'That reminds me vaguely of something, although I didn't have anything to do with the case personally.'

85

'He did one year in prison.'

'Is there the slightest indication that a woman might have come regularly to the flat, including the bedroom?'

'The cupboards have been gone through with a fine tooth-comb, if I may say so. Not a trace of face powder anywhere, no cream, not even a woman's hair.'

'What about the carpet?'

'Dorin is without doubt one of the best authorities in the world on animal or vegetable fibres. He's nuts about them. He spent more than an hour studying the carpet with a magnifying glass and he collected about thirty barely visible threads. He has been working on them for hours. When I say threads, I mean silk threads. They are very old, at least three hundred years old, and Dorin could swear they come from a Chinese rug.

'He is still analysing his find, because he wants to be absolutely accurate.'

Maigret liked the atmosphere of these attic rooms, where the men worked quietly, away from the public gaze.

Each man knew what he had to do. The articulated figure which was used so often in reconstructions stood near one of the gable windows. It was used to discover, for example, in what position a man would be found if he had been struck by a knife in such a way, or if a bullet had followed a particular trajectory.

'If there's anything new tomorrow, tell Janvier. I'll be in Bandol.'

Moers was not the kind of man to take his holidays on the Riviera, and for him Bandol must have been like something in a dream.

'You'll be hot,' was all he murmured.

86

When Maigret announced to his wife at dinner that he was going to Bandol the next day, she smiled and said:

'I knew that already.'

'How?'

'Because the wireless said just a moment ago that although the service would be in the church of Notre Dame de Lorette tomorrow morning, the actual burial would be in Bandol cemetery. What do you expect to discover there?'

'Nothing definite. Perhaps a hint, just something. I'm going there for the same reason that I'm going to the service tomorrow.'

'You'll be hot.'

'I may have to spend the night there. That depends on planes. I can't bring myself to come back to Paris by train.'

'I'll pack your little blue case.'

'Thank you. Just shirts and my toilet bag.'

He felt guilty at going to the Midi at the taxpayers' expense, since it was not absolutely necessary. There was even a chance that he would discover nothing at all.

He slept well, as he almost always did, and was blinded by the sunlight when Madame Maigret brought him his first cup of coffee.

'They say it'll be eighty-six degrees in Marseilles today,' she said, smiling.

'What about Paris?'

'Seventy-eight. The hottest May for thirty-two years.'

'My plane is at twelve something. I'm not sure exactly what, because Janvier saw to the ticket. I'll have just enough time to look in at the Quai before going to Orly.

I'll take my case now.'

'What about your lunch? Where and when will you have your lunch?'

'Oh, on the trot. I'll have a sandwich at the bar at Orly.'

He was going towards the door when she said:

'Aren't you going to give me a kiss?'

He would have come back to do so anyway.

'Don't be worried. I'm not taking a fifty-year-old single-engined plane, and I'm not going round the world.'

He felt a little emotional just the same, as he did each time he left his wife for more than a day.

Once out on the pavement he raised his head, and he knew in advance that he would see her looking out of the window.

It was just as well that he did, for she was holding up the blue case which he had forgotten, and they met half-way up the stairs.

It was quarter past nine when Janvier went into the superintendent's office.

'It seems the street is already full and that the church won't be able to hold everyone.'

Maigret had been expecting something of the kind, but not quite to that extent.

'Still no news of the Flea?'

'No. Blanche Pigoud had a phone call at the Canary last night. When she took her seat at the bar again she seemed excited, but almost immediately afterwards a customer came and sat with her.'

'What time did she go home'

'About four in the morning.'

'Too bad,' Maigret growled to himself.

And he looked up the girl's number, found it and rang. Contrary to his expectations, it was not long before she answered.

'Who is it?' she asked in a sleepy voice.

'Superintendent Maigret.'

'Have you any news?'

'No. You do. Who telephoned you last night at the Canary?'

'You're right. It was him.'

'Did he tell you where he was?'

'No. He wanted to know if you or Inspector Louis were up to date on things concerning him. I said yes. Then he asked me if you were angry, and that time I said no.'

She sounded like a child sluggish with sleep.

'It's true isn't it? You aren't angry with him?'

'Is he still afraid?'

'Yes. He wanted to know, too, if there were any strangers hanging around the house.

' "Has no one been arrested yet?"

' "Not as far as I know."

' "They haven't searched Manuel Mori's place?"

' "I think they have. The superintendent came here with Inspector Louis, but they didn't give me any details. In any case, there's a policeman watching over me day and night." '

'He didn't say anything else?' asked Maigret.

'Only that he was changing his whereabouts every night. That's all. I didn't have time to say much to him, because a customer had been hanging round me for some time.'

89

'Go back to bed and don't be afraid of anything. If you have anything new to tell me during the day, ring Inspector Janvier at the Quai des Orfèvres.'

'Are you going to Bandol?'

He was beginning to be irritated by it. Everyone talked to him about this trip as if he had announced it in the papers.

'There you are!' he sighed, looking at Janvier, who was silhouetted against the green of the trees. 'I don't know if it's a good idea, but he's changing his hiding-place every night.'

'Perhaps it's not so stupid an idea. There must be so many people looking for him ...'

If, as was probable, Mori had given the word, all the layabouts of Montmartre must be looking for the Flea. And he, with his build, could hardly pass unnoticed in a crowd.

'I'll come back in a little while to pick up my case. You'd better give me my plane ticket now.'

Luckily the departure time was later than he had feared: 12.55.

'See you soon.'

He had himself driven to the Rue Ballu and told the policeman who was driving him to wait for him near the church.

More than two hundred people were crowded in front of the house, into which only a few were going to present their condolences. There were people of all kinds, local shopkeepers, pimps, restaurant or nightclub proprietors.

They began to bring the flowers down, and it took two cars to hold them and the wreaths.

Then four men brought down the mahogany coffin, which they slid into the hearse.

The church was quite near; there wouldn't have been enough cars for everyone. When Line Marcia appeared on the doorstep, in full mourning, blonde and pale, there was a movement in the crowd, as if a film star had passed by, and it seemed for a moment as if people were going to applaud.

She took her place in a huge black car which moved along at walking pace. All the staff of the Sardine walked in the first rank. The following rank was formed by old men, men of Monsieur Maurice's age, and some even older.

Very dignified, they walked along bare-headed, while the curious came to the windows to look.

Under a triumphant sun, the procession did not lack style, and Marcia would have been pleased with such a funeral.

When Maigret turned round, he saw that the cortège, all along the streets, was more than three hundred metres long, and the traffic had been rerouted by policemen, who were making feverish gestures with white batons.

'A fantastic funeral!' cried a boy who was passing.

The church was indeed already full except for the first rows, which had been cordoned off from the others with black ropes.

Line walked alone, still at the front, very straight, her blue eyes impenetrable.

She sat alone in the first row, while the employees sat in the second. There were people standing in the two naves. There were more outside and the great doors had been left open, so that one felt the spring breezes.

The organ played a funeral march and a few moments later the service began.

Maigret, standing in the left aisle, was looking at faces and it was not long before he saw Mori's. He had taken his place in the row of important people, people of authority, as if he was there by right, although he was the youngest.

His look met Maigret's and it expressed a kind of defiance.

The superintendent didn't wait until the end of the service. He was hot. He was thirsty. A few minutes later he plunged into the shade of a *bistrot* where he asked for a glass of beer.

'As funerals go, it's a good funeral,' muttered the proprietor, who was very old and whose hand trembled a little. 'Who is it, in fact?'

'The proprietor of the Sardine.'

'At the top of the Rue Fontaine?'

'Yes.'

'I thought it was a gangster.'

'He was, in his younger days.'

Maigret drank his beer in one swallow, paid and went to find the black police car.

'Take me to the Quai.'

'Right, chief.'

It was eleven o'clock. Just time to pick up his suitcase and shake Janvier's hand, then Maigret went to Orly in the same car.

Were Line and Manuel going to travel together? Would the coffin be taken to Bandol by plane?

After the formalities had been gone through, he still

had a little time and he went to look for the superintendent at the airport. This was a man he knew, because he
had worked at the Quai des Orfèvres.

'Are you going to Bandol?'

Maigret had to contain his annoyance.

'Yes. I leave in about twenty minutes, I think.'

'They'll be calling the passengers very soon.'

'Tell me, do you know if a plane has been chartered
to carry a coffin?'

'Monsieur Maurice's?'

'Yes.'

'He's departing with his wife at about three o'clock,
on board a private plane she has rented—him in the box,
her outside, of course.'

Maigret decided not to shrug his shoulders.

'How long will it take them to make the trip?'

'They're to land at Toulon. From there a hearse will
take the coffin to Bandol. It's only fourteen kilometres.'

'Passengers for Marseilles,' the loudspeaker began.

And Maigret went to the door which was pointed out
to him. Ten minutes later the plane, a twin-propellered
machine, took off.

He had promised himself to look at the scenery, because
he was particularly fond of the countryside south of
Lyons. He didn't have the chance, because he was asleep
long before they flew over the Rhône.

From the airport at Marseilles he was taken to the
station; there was a train for Bandol half an hour later.

He felt a little ridiculous with his suitcase on his knees
and his hat, which he kept removing to wipe his forehead.

At Bandol, right from the station platform, the sun

literally burned his skin and he began to regret having come. Taxis were waiting, as was an old fiacre, and Maigret chose the fiacre.

'Where'll I take you, boss?'

'Do you know a good hotel near the sea?'

'I'll have you there in a quarter of an hour.'

The wheels sank a little in the asphalt softened by the heat. The town was almost white, like Algiers, and there were palm trees along some of the avenues.

He saw the sea, flag blue, through the greenery. Then he saw the beach, where only a few people were sunbathing while half a dozen swimmers were swimming. The season had not yet begun.

They passed the Casino. The hotel was white too, with an enormous terrace sprinkled with coloured parasols.

'Have you a room?'

'For how long?'

'Just for one night.'

'A single? You prefer to face the sea?'

He filled up his registration card.

'Room number 233.'

The hotel was called The Tamarisks. It was cool and very clean.

'Can I get a drink somewhere?'

'The bar is in there on the right.'

He went in and drank a glass of beer.

'Aren't you Superintendent Maigret?' the bartender asked him after looking at him for a moment.

He was a young man, very blond, and he blushed at his own daring.

'Are you on the Coast for long?'

'Just till tomorrow.'

'I thought so. You've come for Monsieur Maurice's burial, haven't you?'

'Was he well known around here?'

'You might as well say he was God himself.'

'Is his villa far from here?'

'About a quarter of an hour on foot. It's almost at the other end of the sea-front, not far from the villa of the late Raimu. You'll recognize it because it has an enormous swimming pool beside it.'

Maigret still had the feeling of cheating, of taking an unauthorized holiday.

'And the cemetery?'

'Less than a kilometre from the villa. There's going to be a lot of people there, you know. They've been arriving from Toulon and Marseilles since this morning.'

'What kind of people?'

'Important people. I even wonder whether the sub-prefect won't come. Some people say so.'

Maigret swallowed a second beer and, after consulting his watch, started to walk. Luckily the avenues along the sea-front were shady.

The plane must have unloaded the coffin, and Line, at Toulon. The further he walked, the more people he saw, and when he turned a corner, there was almost the same sight as in the Rue Ballu that morning.

How many of those people knew the truth? It didn't matter, for none of them would tell it.

Only one person had, from a public call-box, without even giving his name, and he had gone to ground heaven knew where in Montmartre.

Just on the edge of the crowd he saw a face he knew well.
It was Boutang, superintendent of the Police Judiciaire
in Toulon.

'It's funny,' Boutang said, shaking him by the hand.
'I thought of you this morning when I was shaving, and
I had a feeling that you would come.'

He pointed to the crowd.

'What do you think of that? What a haul we could
make. Not only is the cream of all the villains of Toulon
there, but also those of Marseilles, Cannes, and Nice...'

Someone came up to them and Boutang shook his
hand, making introductions.

'Charmeroy, superintendent of police in Bandol. I
suppose you recognized Superintendent Maigret,
Charmeroy?'

'Glad to meet you.'

They were both big men. Men who knew their business
and who didn't let themselves be intimidated.

'Nine-tenths of those here live on the fringes of the
law, and the extraordinary thing is that there isn't one
against whom we have any proof.'

'When Marcia lived in Bandol in the summer, did he
have many guests?'

'No, very few. A few close friends. The Mori brothers
in particular '

'Did they sleep at the villa?'

'Yes. And as if by chance, it was always at the time of the big burglaries. You must have read about them in the papers. Summer residents who have a big villa on the Coast, who have a yacht too and take a cruise to the Greek islands in July or August—when they get back they are very surprised at not being able to find their furniture and their valuables.'

'Just like the châteaux.'

'More or less. I suspected the Mori brothers and even the big man, whom everyone round here calls Monsieur Maurice. I had the villa watched. As if by chance, every time there was a robbery the Moris didn't leave the villa, but played gin-rummy with Marcia into the small hours. Do you know his wife? She has a bit of class and you'd think she'd be out of her depth in that atmosphere.'

The funeral procession arrived. Behind the hearse Line sat alone in a car, then there were other cars with Riviera licence plates. Some big American cars, but also the fast sports cars of the younger set.

It all moved at walking pace and there was another crowd which followed as best it could.

There was a moment of confusion. The driver of the hearse, when he drew near to the villa, was on the point of turning right, but the master of ceremonies rushed up to give him other instructions.

The two groups mixed. It seemed as if everyone knew everyone else. They shook hands. Some spoke in whispers.

Madame Marcia got out of the car and went to the villa. She had changed since the morning. She was now

97

wearing a black suit of lightweight material and a white silk hat. Her gloves were white too.

What had she come to do, alone, in the villa? Maigret could find no plausible answer to that question. Nor could Boutang or the local superintendent.

She stayed away less than ten minutes and got back into the car. The procession made a half-turn, entered the Rue des Ecoles, then the Avenue du 11 Novembre, where they straightaway found themselves at the gates of the cemetery.

Confusion reigned again, for many people ran across the graves to get a good place near the open pit.

A priest was there and greeted Line.

She was not weeping, any more than she had wept that morning at the Church of Notre Dame de Lorette. The heavy coffin was lowered. The priest mumbled a few prayers, then the flowers were laid in readiness on the neighbouring tombs.

'All the top mobsters are there. The young ones too, proud to be seen with them. What are you going to do now, superintendent?'

'I don't know.'

'Where are you staying?'

'At the Tamarisks.'

'It's very good and the owners are nice people.'

Line had already taken a car to the villa. Maigret, in the crowd, hadn't seen Manuel Mori or his brother.

'I think I'm going to make a visit.'

'Do you think she was in on things?'

'I don't think. I'm certain. Unfortunately, I have no proof.'

'Good luck. If you need me, you know where to find me, and where to find Charmeroy.'

The crowd dispersed little by little and headed for the centre of town to quench its thirst in the bars. Only a few cars, those of the more important people, went directly to Toulon or Marseilles.

Maigret found himself alone in front of the white villa. It was not of enormous size. It was a pretty villa, nothing more, the most striking thing about it being the swimming pool surrounded by deck chairs. The garden consisted of a few palm trees, many cacti and vaguely tropical plants which Maigret was not familiar with.

He took the steps in three strides, rang the bell and was surprised to see the door open immediately and Line standing in front of him.

'I might have guessed that you wouldn't miss the chance. You have no respect for mourning, have you?'

'What about you?'

They went straight into a huge hall with white walls where the furniture and furnishings had as much class, though in a different style, as those in the old house in the Rue Ballu.

She did not ask him to sit down. She waited, standing, for him to start the conversation. The hand holding her cigarette trembled a little.

'I want to talk to you about the night your husband died.'

'I thought I had already answered you on that subject.'

'Since you didn't tell the truth, I shall ask you the question again.'

99

And Maigret sat down in one of the cream leather armchairs.

'You're taking advantage of the fact that I'm not strong enough to throw you out.'

'You wouldn't dare do that anyway. If only so as not to implicate your lover.'

She turned pale with rage and stubbed out her cigarette in an ashtray.

'Have you no humanity?'

'I have more than enough, in fact. But that depends on who I am talking to. You obviously married Marcia for his money.'

'That's my business.'

She sat down at last, crossed her legs, and lit a fresh cigarette, which she took out of a gold box lying on the table.

'You were in bed, you and Manuel. Someone knocked loudly at the door and I imagine Mori put on a dressing-gown while you wrapped yourself in the sheets.'

She didn't turn a hair. Her face was now impassive. One might even have sworn that there was nothing but curiosity in her pale blue eyes.

'And then?'

'It was your husband.'

'And what did he do, do you think? Did he shake hands with Manuel?'

'He took his gun out of his pocket.'

'Just like a film . . .'

'What I want to know is where Mori's gun was. In some piece of furniture, certainly. But it could as easily have been in the bedroom as in the drawing-room.'

100

'You must first prove that there was a gun in the flat.'

She lit her cigarette.

'And that I was there. And that there was a visitor who was none other than my husband. You've started badly, superintendent.'

Maigret was going to answer when she said, in a voice hardly any louder:

'Come in, dear.'

And immediately a door opened and Manuel appeared, in shorts and espadrilles, as if he had come from the beach.

'Well, superintendent, you do get around, don't you?'

His gaze ran insolently over Maigret from head to foot, then he went to the bar and poured himself a Tom Collins.

'Do you want one too, my dear?'

'I *am* thirsty.'

'What about you, copper?'

'No.'

'As you like. It's useless for you to show me your little yellow paper here. You're well out of your territory.'

'I could get a warrant to take evidence without any difficulty.'

'But you won't.'

'Why not?'

'Because you have nothing against me.'

'Not even the Flea's evidence?'

'Have you found him?'

Manuel frowned.

'The Flea is undoubtedly the one man, if you can call him that, who knows the 9th and 18th *arrondissements* best. The people know him too, and most of them are ready to lay their hands on him. You won't be the one to find him, superintendent. My men will. But you won't have any proof of that, either. You see, I'm putting my cards on the table.

'If we had witnesses here, I would swear once more that I didn't shoot, that no shot was fired in my flat and that Maurice didn't set foot there that night.

'We would repeat too, Line and I, that there had never been anything between us and I defy you to produce people who could say the contrary in court.'

He was not acting. He was swollen with arrogance and Maigret wondered unhappily at the reason for his assurance. He seemed to fear nothing now and Line was as calm as if a man called Marcia had never existed.

The superintendent suddenly thought of the Flea. Had Mori's men, as he called them, finally got their hands on the midget? Had they fixed him so that he would not be dangerous any more, so that he would keep quiet once and for all?

Maigret filled his pipe, lit it, stood up and began to walk about the room.

'I am in fact out of my jurisdiction. I can't use the documents I showed you in Paris ...'

'Exactly.'

'It would only need a phone call for Superintendent Boutang to be here in half an hour with a search warrant. I suppose you know Boutang?'

'He's no friend of mine.'

'Well, it's up to you. Either you allow me to look through the villa or I ring Toulon.'

102

'Look over it, do. As long as you don't take anything away.'

In the big drawing-room itself, the superintendent made a discovery. One of the walls was filled with a bookcase in which, as in Paris, all the books were richly bound.

Now, on the lower shelves there were piles of magazines. Not at all such weeklies as are found in any kiosk, they didn't square with Monsieur Maurice's character. Maigret read out their titles in a low voice, establishing that they had at least been leafed through.

'*Farms and Châteaux* ... Very interesting reading, isn't it? *Country Life ... Knowledge of Art ...*'

Mori frowned and glanced at his mistress.

'They're mine,' she said. 'I don't play cards, and when the men play gin rummy, I sit in a corner and read.'

The next room was a dining-room in the old Provençal style, and on the left was a boudoir in which every piece of furniture, as in Paris, could have taken its place in a museum.

'Is it genuine?' Maigret asked, pointing to a Van Gogh. It was the woman who answered.

'I'm not an expert, but my husband didn't usually buy fakes.'

The kitchen was vast, modern, spotless.

'And yet you had few guests.'

'How do you know?'

'I've had time to get information. I also know that the Mori brothers spent on average a month a year with you.'

'They were my husband's best friends.'

103

'He probably didn't know anything about your relationship with Manuel.'

Manuel still hadn't turned a hair and was listening to Maigret without saying a word.

'You're wrong. My husband was sixty-two and had had a good life. In one sense he was worn out. He was perhaps in love with me when he married me five years ago, but it wasn't long before we began to live like brother and sister.'

'You can go on lying. It doesn't bother me.'

He climbed a marble staircase and pushed open a double door, which opened into a vast bedroom ending in a terrace overlooking the sea.

'Your room?'

There were twin beds and yet more superb furniture. The bathroom was even bigger than the one in the Rue Ballu and completely lined in yellow marble.

'Just one bathroom for the two of you. That doesn't fit in with your story of brother and sister.'

'You can think what you like.'

There were two other bedrooms upstairs, each with a bathroom.

'The Mori brothers, I suppose.'

'Guestrooms.'

'Apart from them, were there many other guests to use these rooms?'

'It happened.'

The pictures were almost all old ones, whose painters Maigret didn't recognize.

'Is there a loft?'

'No. Mansard attics, where the servants sleep.'

104

'Are they here just now?'

'No. I'm going away again this evening. A cleaning-woman is all that is needed to keep the villa in order.'

'And you invariably engage different staff each year.'

'We do change, yes.'

'So that for most of the year this house is empty at night and there is no one to keep an eye on it.'

She nodded. Then he rapped at her, not without irony:

'Are you afraid of burglars?'

'They wouldn't dare touch my husband's house.'

'Nor yours, now that you have inherited it.'

When they got back to the drawing-room, Maigret did not move towards the door, but sat down again in the armchair he had previously occupied.

The couple looked at each other.

'I must point out to you that our aeroplane is waiting for us at Toulon.'

'*Your* plane. You used the plural. Does that mean that Mori is going to travel with you?'

'Why not?'

'As a friend. With the most honourable intentions.'

'It's time to change that record now. It's true, we are lovers.'

'That's better.'

'It's not a crime.'

'Except when the husband gets a heavy-calibre bullet in the chest.'

He turned to Mori.

'We didn't finish our little conversation on that subject just now. We were at the point where, having put on a dressing-gown in a hurry, you were going to the door. You opened it, of course.'

'And then?'

'I'm waiting to hear the next bit from you. Maurice Marcia didn't stay on the doorstep.'

'Did I tell you it was him?'

'Let's say you didn't deny it. He didn't sit down in the living-room and have a chat. On the contrary, he went right through it to the bedroom.

'He only needed to lift up the sheet to find his wife as naked as a worm ...'

'What delicacy!' remarked Line ironically.

'In fact, from the moment he came in he knew what he was going to find. He already knew it when he left the Sardine.'

'He had known about it for three years.'

'No. You won't make me believe that he was a complaisant husband, nor that he was impotent. He probably had his gun in his hand. You, Mori, you had your gun in the pocket of your dressing-gown. Where did you get it from?'

'I had no gun in the flat.'

'In that case, who did the shooting? Marcia's gun wasn't used. As for the gun which killed him, it's probably at the bottom of the Seine.'

'You should send skin divers down for it, then.'

Maigret pursued his train of thought without letting himself be discouraged.

'Supposing you went to the door without a gun, which is possible ...'

'At last!'

'I haven't finished. You picked up a gun when you saw Marcia going to the bedroom. Unless the gun was in the bedside table and some good soul handed it to you so that you could defend yourself.'

'I'd like to hear you tell that to the jury at the assizes.'

'There's another possibility . . .'

'What is it? You're making me curious.'

'That it wasn't you who killed him.'

'So another character comes on the scene to play the villain.'

'No. Line had all the time in the world, when you went to the door, to get the gun which was in the bedside table. And when Marcia threatened you, she . . .'

'She would certainly have hit the ceiling, because she has never used a firearm in her life.'

'We'll talk about that later.'

'In Paris, right.'

'This time it will be in my office.'

'Why not?'

'You may come out of it with handcuffs on.'

'It's not very elegant of you to try to impress me. And if I should leave France before that?'

'Interpol would waste no time finding you. You forget you have a record, and besides, you're quite conspicuous.

'I suppose you two intend to get married after some time has passed?'

'It's possible.'

'Go and catch your plane then.'

Manuel joked:

'Don't you want a seat?'

Maigret looked at him with the calm he had had all

afternoon, but one could sense that it was the calm preceding the storm.

He ate bouillabaisse in a tidy little restaurant, alone in his corner. He didn't get as much pleasure from it as he had hoped, which must have been due to his state of mind.

Night had fallen. The tree-lined promenades facing the sea were softly lit and one could hear the soft swish of the waves.

He sat down on a bench. The air was soft. He felt lazy. It wouldn't have taken much for him to have had Madame Maigret come from Paris, and they would have spent a week's holiday in Bandol.

He went to bed early and fell asleep straight away. He had to get up early the next day to catch his plane at Marseilles, and he landed at Orly at ten-thirty.

He took a taxi and had it take him home first. His wife did not welcome him with great raptures of joy, but one could tell from her beaming face that she had come alive again.

'You aren't too tired?'

'A little.'

'Would you like me to make some coffee for you?'

'No, thank you. I have to go to the Quai.'

'Still this damnable case?'

'This damnable case, as you say.'

'The papers yesterday spoke of you. They say you're being mysterious, that you are worried, even discouraged, and that you are certainly hiding something.'

'If they only knew the truth! I don't know if I'll be back for lunch. That depends on what's waiting for me at the office. By the way, we must go to Bandol together sometime.'

He got into the little taxi parked in front of the building and a little later he climbed up the big staircase at the Quai. On his desk were already piled administrative documents, reports and several letters. He opened the door of the inspectors' office and called Janvier.

'Had a good trip, chief?'

'Not bad. Guess who was in the villa even before Madame Marcia?'

'Mori, of course.'

'Exactly. He's a hard case, believe me, and he'll lead us a merry dance before we get him to tell us anything.'

'I have some good news for you. Well, half-good. Inspector Louis phoned this morning. He missed the Flea by a few hours and he wants to talk to you about it. He'll stay in his office all morning so that you can ring him.'

'Do that for me. Tell him I'll come and see him.'

He went and stood in front of the window and rediscovered 'his' Paris with as much joy as if he had been away from it for weeks. There was a storm in the air, but it probably wouldn't break before evening.

'He's waiting for you.'

'Are you coming with me? That'll let us talk on the way.'

And he did indeed, as they were going, put Janvier in the picture about everything that had happened in Bandol. They stopped for a moment in front of the police station in the Place Saint Georges and Monsieur Louis, as some people called him formally, to tease him, joined them in the car straight away.

'Do you want to see the last place where he was hiding?'

'Yes.'

'Then stop right up at the top of Montmartre, in the Place du Tertre.'

There were artists all along the pavements, and the little tables with red-checked tablecloths were ready for the tourists.

'Turn the corner into the Rue du Mont-Cenis and park the car at the side of the road.'

Lower down the street there were newish blocks of flats but in the upper part most of the houses had kept their old-fashioned character. Inspector Louis took them into an alleyway between two buildings, which had a glass-fronted workshop at the end.

Louis knocked. A loud voice cried:

'Come in!'

They found themself in a sculptor's studio, and the sculptor was looking at the superintendent with his eyes half-closed, as he would have looked at a model.

'You, you're Superintendent Maigret. Am I wrong?'

'You're not wrong.'

'What about him?'

'Inspector Janvier.'

'It's years since I've had so many people in my studio.'

He had white hair, a little beard and white moustaches, and his cheeks were as rosy as a baby's.

'Monsieur Sorel is the oldest artist on the Butte,' explained Inspector Louis. 'How many years did you tell me you'd been in this studio?'

'Fifty-three years. I've seen them come and go, artists,

110

starting with Picasso, with whom I often had a bite to eat...'

He had a rather naïve, childish look. Looking around the studio, one couldn't have had any illusions about his talent. He only sculpted children's heads, the head of the same child, it seemed, with different expressions; undoubtedly these busts were sold at the art dealer's in the Place du Tertre.

'I believe you've had the Flea with you.'

'For two days and two nights. He left yesterday evening, at nightfall. He didn't dare stay any longer in the same place for fear of being seen.'

'How did he happen to choose your studio?'

'What if I were to tell you that I knew him when he was only fifteen? He was a street urchin then, getting along as best he could, and not often getting enough to fill his belly.

'Meeting him one day in the Place du Tertre, I asked him if he would like to pose for me, and he came. I remember the bust I made of him, one of my best. It's now in God knows what collection. Because of his grimacing expression and his enormous mouth I made a clown more real than if I'd had a professional clown as a model.

'He was a good lad. From time to time he would knock on my door, particularly in the winter, and ask if he could sleep on my mattress. It was my dog's mattress, because I had a dog then, a big Saint Bernard, but that's another story.'

'Did he tell you about his troubles?'

'He asked me if I could hide him for a night or two. I wanted to know if he was hiding from the police. He

111

told me that on the contrary, he was very well in with Inspector Louis and Superintendent Maigret. He added that that was precisely why some people were trying to lay their hands on him.'

'He didn't tell you where he was going when he left here?'

'No. As far as I could tell, it's not far away. He doesn't appear to want to go far from this area.'

'During these two days, he didn't talk to you about anyone in particular?'

'Yes, he did. A former policeman, now retired, who was good to him when he was a boy. I don't know his name. I don't know him at all. I only go out of my studio to do my shopping, less than a hundred metres from here, and to take my work to the dealer.'

Only then did he seem to notice that they were all standing.

'Forgive me for not asking you to sit down, but I haven't enough chairs or stools. And as for offering you a drink, I only have rough red, the same stuff Utrillo drank, which would probably be too strong for you.'

'During these two days and nights, did he go out?'

'No. But he was surprised and very happy to find that I have the telephone. He rang a woman to tell her how he was, and I went to smoke my pipe discreetly in the courtyard.

'All I can tell you is that he was very afraid. He couldn't keep still. He jumped up at every noise, and he asked me at least ten times if I ever had any visitors. Who would come to see me? I don't even want a cleaning-woman.'

Maigret warmed to him, for he was indeed one of the

rare specimens of old Montmartre still living.

'Oh! He mentioned you. It seems you ought to arrest someone, but he can't understand why you are taking so long.

' "If the superintendent doesn't hurry, he'll have no one to be a witness, because they'll have got me before then." '

As he went out, after shaking hands with the old man, Maigret muttered to himself:

'A retired policeman.'

'I've already begun to work on that track,' said Inspector Louis with his usual impassiveness. 'It's likely to be a policeman from the 18th *arrondissement*, or perhaps the 9th, because he wouldn't have come far to live ... It appears, too, that that's the neighbourhood the Flea frequented most when he was a boy.

'I have begun to study the lists of policemen who retired in the last ten years. I haven't found any yet who live in Montmartre, but I'll go on with it this afternoon.'

It would have been easier, obviously, in a district where everyone knew everyone else, to ask the first old lady they met, or the grocer, but might that not have been dangerous for the Flea?

'Where shall I drop you?'

'Nowhere. I'm going to stay round here.'

He had his methods. He was a kind of hunting dog, and he would have been unhappy if he had had to work in a team. He was no doubt going to make the rounds of the bars again, flooding his stomach with quarter-bottles of Vichy while listening to the conversations around him.

'To Blanche Pigoud's, in the Rue Fromentin.'

Maigret too was beginning to worry about the fate of

113

the Flea, but it wouldn't have done any good to put ten men, or twenty, to look for him.

'By the way, are the Mori brothers still being followed?'

'The detectives are taking turns. While his brother was away, Jo spent a lot of time in the Rue du Caire, then went off in a lorry, so that it was impossible for the detective to follow him. He came back, without any crates, at about eight in the evening. He closed the steel door and went back to his flat to take a shower and change. Do you know where he had dinner?'

'Yes. At the Sardine.'

'How did you guess?'

'Because it was already a sort of takeover.'

'What about Manuel?'

'Even easier. He dined at the Sardine too, with Line. It's probably the first time she had eaten in her husband's restaurant. Poor Marcia didn't guess she would soon be the owner.'

'You'd think they were behaving like this out of defiance. I'm sure the staff was indignant to see her on the day of the funeral with the Mori brothers.'

'Manuel doesn't give a damn what the staff thinks. If the employees leave, he'll replace them by his own men. That's probably his intention. I'll bet he slept at the Rue Ballu.'

'You win your bet. As far as I know, he's still there.'

'There's something wrong somewhere,' Maigret thought out loud.

'The Flea?'

'The Flea's no use to us unless we can get our hands

114

on him. No! There's a flaw somewhere else and I'm getting a headache from trying to work it out.'

'Shall I come up with you?'

'Better not. In spite of her profession, the girl is quite shy. With me, she's already at ease, but if we both go...'

This time the Flea's girlfriend was up, taking her breakfast by the window.

'A cup of coffee. There's some made.'

'Well, yes, then.'

She seemed worried.

'Do you have any news, superintendent?'

'I know where he spent the last two nights, but he went off yesterday evening.'

'What district was he in?'

'Near the Place du Tertre, with an old sculptor.'

'That's funny. He told me about him once when we went to have dinner just below the Sacré Cœur. It reminded him of his childhood. He described to me the mattress on which he used to sleep, which had once been used by a big dog.'

'He didn't talk to you about anyone else in the neighbourhood?'

'I don't remember. I don't think so.'

'A former policeman, for example?'

'No, really, that means nothing to me.'

'Has he rung you?'

'Twice.'

'What did he say?'

'He's more and more afraid. He can't understand why you aren't arresting the Mori brothers. Their gang

115

would keep quiet then and Justin could breathe freely.'

'Is he angry with me?'

'A little, I think, yes. He's angry with Inspector Louis, too. I told him what you said to me.'

'Listen. There's every chance he may ring you again, unless there's no telephone where he is. Tell him to ring me. I'll give him all the assurances he wants.'

'Is that true?'

'I need to see him, and it is probable that two hours after that, the Mori brothers will be behind bars.'

'I'll tell him. I'll do what I can. Put yourself in my place. He doesn't believe in anything, or anyone, any more.'

A quarter of an hour later, Maigret and Janvier were sitting at the bar in the Sardine. It was the time when they were setting the tables for lunch and the head waiter, by the cash-desk, was taking telephone reservations.

'A beer, Freddy?'

'What about you?' Freddy asked Janvier.

'The same.'

'We don't have anything but imported beer.'

'It doesn't matter.'

It appeared that he was serving them against his will, and he glanced frequently at the door, as if he was afraid to see the Mori brothers come in.

'I've never seen so many people at a funeral,' murmured Maigret, as if to force him to speak.

'There were a lot of people, yes.'

'And there were almost as many in Bandol. People came from everywhere, Nice, Cannes, Toulon, Marseilles ... And the cars! I counted no less than five Ferraris.'

To keep himself in countenance, Freddy was wiping the glasses. Comitat, the head-waiter, had put down the telephone and instead of coming over to them, he stayed at the other end of the room, apparently ignoring them.

Maigret said, with irony:

'Chilly in here today.'

The thermometer must have been registering eighty degrees in the shade.

'Yes, it's chilly.'

'Well, have you seen the boss yet?'

'What boss?'

'Line Marcia. She had dinner here yesterday evening with the Mori brothers. Of course Manuel's really the boss...'

'Listen, Monsieur Maigret, I don't mix myself up in your business. Don't you get mixed up in things here. First of all, if anyone sees me talking to you, that could be bad for me. It might also not do you any good.'

The superintendent and Janvier looked at each other.

'Will you wait here a moment, Janvier?'

And he went off in the direction of the toilets. To get to them, he had to pass near Comitat.

'Bonjour, Monsieur Raoul,' he said.

'Freddy should have told you you're not welcome here.'

'He did. Change of management. And suddenly everyone in the place is jittery.'

'I'd be obliged if you wouldn't come back again.'

'You're forgetting it's a public place and it's open to

117

anyone who is decently dressed and has enough money.'

He went to the toilets, and back to the bar. It was a little after quarter past twelve.

'You know what we're going to do, Janvier? We're going to have lunch here.'

They went towards the nearest table. Comitat rushed up.

'I'm sorry, but this table is taken.'

'Then we'll take the next one.'

'It's taken too. All the tables are taken.'

'Let's say, in that case, that this one is taken by me. Sit down, Janvier.'

It wasn't malice on Maigret's part. He was furious, and he wanted to make them fume in their turn.

'The menu, please. And don't forget that I could have this place closed down in twenty-four hours.'

The menu was immense, with the wine list on the back.

'There are *coquilles Saint-Jacques*, Janvier. What do you say to that?'

'*Coquilles Saint-Jacques*, fine.'

'Followed by braised rib of beef.'

'That's fine too.'

He handed back the menu.

'A light wine ... A Beaujolais?'

'I'm agreeable to that.'

The head-waiter stood behind them as straight as a pike-staff. Then four customers came in and sat down near the window. The little dark cashier had taken her seat, but Maigret tried in vain to catch her eye. She appeared not to recognize him.

118

Monsieur Maurice was dead. When he was alive no one made a wrong move, but there was still something mellow in the atmosphere.

Yesterday evening Mori had come to take possession of the place, in company with Madame Marcia, and they had all understood.

From now on they would all have to tread carefully. They had begun to do so. They just managed to falter a few excuses when they met for the first time.

'What do you bet we won't be served inside half an hour, if not an hour?'

And in fact the table for four was served before them, then two English people who had only just come in. The room filled up bit by bit, and the more they delayed in serving them, the more Maigret smiled, smoking his pipe ostentatiously.

'Don't hurry!' He said to the head-waiter, who was passing.

'No, monsieur. I don't intend to.'

The Moris did not turn up, and the two men finally had something to eat and drink.

When Maigret got back to the Quai it was after three o'clock, and the first person he saw was the eternal Inspector Louis sitting on one of the benches in the corridor, his black hat on his knees.

The superintendent had him come into his office, and Louis sat down once more on the edge of a chair.

'I think I've been lucky, Superintendent.'

He had the soft voice of a shy man, and he rarely looked the person he was speaking to in the face.

'When I left you this morning, I began to go round the bars and cafés again, at the top of Montmartre, around the Place du Tertre. I know, it's a mania of mine. I came to the Trois Tonneaux, a regular's *bistrot* in the Rue Gabrielle. I stayed at the counter as usual, and I took my usual quarter-bottle of Vichy.'

Maigret knew that it would be no use to hurry him. The inspector spoke with the slowness and concern for exactitude which were part of his character.

'In a corner, under a clock with an advertisement on it, four men were playing *belote*. They were all fairly old, and they had probably been playing their game in the same place, at the same time, for many years.

'I jumped when I heard one of them say:

' "Your turn, *brigadier*."

'The man he was talking to must have been between

seventy and seventy-five, but he was still youthful.

'Three times, in the space of ten minutes, they spoke to him, giving him the title of *brigadier*.

' "Was he a policeman?" I asked the proprietor in a low voice.

' "He was one for forty years. A real policeman, of the old school. He was a familiar figure in the district, and he was like a father to the children."

' "Has he been retired for long?"

' "Ten years at least, and he comes in every day for his game. He lives alone, now that his son is married and lives in Meaux. His daughter is a nurse at the Bichat Hospital and there's another son, I don't know what he does, nothing particularly good, I think."

' "Does he live far from here?"

' "Not very far. In the Rue Tholozé. Right opposite the only dance-hall in the street. His wife died five years ago and he does his own cooking and cleaning. We have a lot of them around here, old men and women who live alone on a small pension." '

Maigret knew Montmartre well enough to know that it is a town within a town. Some people never went beyond the Place Clichy.

'Have you got his exact address?'

'I left the *bistrot* so that I wouldn't attract attention. The man came out half an hour later and stopped at the butcher's to buy two chops.

'I followed him to the Rue Tholozé, at some distance, because he would know all about being followed. He went into a three-storey building just opposite the Tam-Tam, a dance-hall. I rang the police station of the 18th *arron-*

121

dissement to ask for the help of a detective for an hour or two. One of the young ones came, and he is keeping watch not far from the house.'

Now he was silent. He had said everything, in his own way.

'Did you hear that, Janvier?'

For Janvier had come into the office at the same time as the superintendent.

'Shall we go?'

'Of course.'

'Shall we take any men with us?'

'There's no point. We have to carry it off as discreetly as possible.'

They took one of the little black cars which were parked in the courtyard of the Police Judiciaire.

'The Rue Tholozé isn't a one-way street?'

'It's bound to be, because it ends in a flight of steps.'

They saw from afar the young policeman, who was standing well away from the house.

'I'll go in alone,' said Maigret. 'There's no point in scaring him.'

He spoke to the concierge, showing his police badge.

'Is the *brigadier* at home?'

'Monsieur Colson? Of course, everyone still calls him the *brigadier*. He came in about two hours ago. He's probably taking his nap now.'

'What floor?'

'Second floor, the door on the left.'

There was no lift, of course. It was an old house, like almost all the houses in the street, and a thick smell of cooking hung in the stairwell.

122

There was no doorbell, and Maigret knocked at the door.

'Come in,' said a deep voice.

It was a small flat, filled with the furniture which had once furnished a whole house. In the bedroom on the right there were two beds, one of which had undoubtedly been used by successive children.

There were two, or three, of everything. There was no refrigerator, but a wire-netting meat-safe hung out of the window.

'It isn't possible! Superintendent Maigret in my house! Come in, do. There's someone here who'll be very pleased to see you.'

He showed the superintendent into a stuffy room which served as both dining-room and living-room. A man not five feet tall and looking like a child whose face had been accidentally wrinkled, was looking anxiously at the visitor.

'Have you arrested him?' he asked before anything else.

'Not yet, but you're safe.'

Brigadier Colson interrupted.

'I've told him at least ten times that he ought to call you and tell you where he was. He was trembling when he came here. He is terrified of these Mori brothers, is that their name? They hadn't been heard of in my time.'

'They're barely thirty years old.'

'I watch the television in the evening, but I don't read the papers. Justin remembered me. I knew him when he hung about this neighbourhood, when he only had old espadrilles on his feet.'

'What are you going to do with me?'

123

The Flea was tense and could not relax.

'We'll both go to the Quai des Orfèvres. In my office we'll talk, just you and me. Most probably, after we have talked, the Mori brothers will be arrested.'

'How did you find me?'

'It was Inspector Louis who got on your trail.'

'The others could have done as much.'

'Thank you for the hospitality you've given him, *brigadier*, and I hope the chops were good.'

'How did you know ... ?'

'Inspector Louis again. And have a good game of *belote* tomorrow morning!'

He turned to the midget, who still hadn't relaxed.

'Come on.'

The retired policeman took them to the door and watched them go downstairs, not without a certain melancholy.

'Get into the car.'

The Flea found himself in the back with Inspector Louis.

'And I thought I was so well hidden,' Justin sighed.

'It was only by chance that I got on the trail of the *brigadier*.'

He kept as far away from the door as possible, afraid of being seen from outside.

They went together up the stairs of the Police Judiciaire, which the Flea looked at with a kind of respect tinged with fear. Maigret wondered which course to take —to have all three of them in his office, or to question Justin Crotton alone.

He decided on the latter course.

124

'I'll see you shortly,' he said to Louis and Janvier. 'Come on in.'

He stopped himself just in time from saying 'boy'.

'Sit down. Do you smoke?'

'Yes.'

'Have you any cigarettes?'

'I have two left.'

'Have this packet.'

Maigret always had two or three packets in his drawer for interviews.

'What do you . . . ?'

'Just a minute.'

For there was a note on his desk.

'The laboratory would like you to phone them.'

He rang Moers.

'You've got something?'

'Yes. The laboratory has done its work well. The textile man went to the best carpet merchant in Paris. His first impressions were confirmed. The silk threads come from an old Chinese rug. It must date from the sixteenth or seventeenth century. In France there can't be any more than three or four outside museums.

'The merchant doesn't know who owns them. He's going to check on it. There's something else more important. There were tiny traces of blood on the carpet, where the rug had been. The blood was very diluted with water. They must have washed and rewashed the stain, with a teazle brush, because they also found a piece of teazle.'

'Is it possible to tell what blood group it belongs to?'

'That's been done. Group AB.'

'Unfortunately, no one thought of checking Monsieur Maurice's blood group before it was too late. Unless the forensic surgeon ...'

'Yes. Perhaps he thought of it. Have you had his report?'

'He doesn't mention it.'

The Flea was looking at the superintendent as if he couldn't yet believe what was happening to him. But why couldn't he relax? What was he still afraid of?

Maigret opened the door.

'Janvier, try to get on to the forensic surgeon as soon as you can. Ask him for me if he thought of analysing Marcia's blood. If he hasn't done so, get him to tell you what they did with his clothes.'

There were about twenty inspectors typing reports, and in the middle of them Louis was sitting erect on a chair, his hat on his knees.

Back in his office, the superintendent spoke to the Flea.

'Now let's see. What time is it? Four o'clock. It's likely we'll find your friend at home.'

And in fact he did hear Blanche Pigoud's voice at the other end of the line.

'Is that you, Justin?'

'No. This is Superintendent Maigret.'

'Have you any news?'

'He's in my office.'

'Did he go there of his own accord?'

'No. I had to look for him.'

'Where was he?'

'In Montmartre, as I expected.'

126

'Have you arrested the ...'

'The Mori brothers. No. One thing at a time. Here's Justin.' He signalled him to take the receiver.

'Hello. Is that you?'

He was awkward, overcome.

'I don't know yet. I've hardly been here a quarter of an hour, and no one's asked me any questions yet. Yes, I'm well. No, I don't know when I'll be back. Goodbye.'

'You won't have to wait long for him,' Maigret said, taking the receiver which was held out to him. 'You can be reassured, anyway.'

After hanging up, he slowly smoked his pipe, carefully watching Justin Crotton. He could not understand the nervousness the Flea still showed.

'Do you always tremble like that?'

'No.'

'What are you afraid of in my office just now? Of me?'

'Perhaps.'

'Why?'

'Because you frighten me. Everything to do with the police frightens me.'

'And yet as a last resort you went to a former policeman to find refuge.'

'As far as I'm concerned, *Brigadier* Colson isn't a real policeman. I knew him when I was hardly sixteen, and it's thanks to him that I was never charged with vagrancy.'

'While I ...?'

'You're so important.'

'How did you know that Line Marcia was Manuel's mistress?'

127

'In the *boîtes* of the district everyone knew.'

'And for three years Monsieur Maurice knew nothing?'

'So it seems.'

'You aren't sure?'

'It's always the person concerned who doesn't know anything, isn't it? Monsieur Maurice was a rich, influential man. I don't think anyone would have dared to say to his face:

'"Your wife is deceiving you with one of your friends."'

'Were Marcia and the Mori brothers friends?'

'For some years, yes.'

'How do you know?'

'Because the Mori brothers went regularly to the Sardine and Monsieur Maurice would sit at their table. They would stay there after it closed.'

'Did they go to the Rue Ballu too?'

'I've seen them go in several times.'

'When Marcia was at home?'

'Yes.'

'How do you know all that?'

'Because I wander around here and there. I have big ears. I listen to what people are saying. Nobody pays any attention to me.'

'Did you often go to the Sardine?'

'To the bar, yes. Freddy is almost a mate of mine.'

'I don't think he will be any more.'

'On the evening of the murder I was in the Rue Fontaine when Monsieur Maurice rushed out suddenly, at an hour which was quite unusual for him.'

'What time was that?'

128

'Just after midnight. He didn't take his car and he hurriedly walked to the Square La Bruyère.'

'Did you know his wife was in Manuel's flat?'

'Yes.'

'How did you know she was there that particular evening?'

'Because I had followed her there.'

'In fact, your passion is to follow people and watch them.'

'I've always dreamed of being a policeman. My height stopped me. Also perhaps my lack of education.'

'Right. You're following Monsieur Maurice. He goes into Manuel's. Was there any light at the windows?'

'Yes.'

'How long had Line been there?'

'About an hour.'

'You didn't go into the building?'

'No.'

'Did you know what was going to happen?'

'Yes. Except I didn't know which one of them would be killed.'

'Did you hear the shot?'

'No. Nor did the other tenants, unless they thought it was a car backfiring.'

'Go on.'

'After about a quarter of an hour Madame Marcia came out of the flat and ran back home.'

'Did you follow her?'

'No. I thought I'd stay.'

'What happened then?'

'A car came rushing up and I was almost caught. It was

the other Mori brother, Jo. His brother must have rung him and told him to come round in a hurry.'

Maigret was following this narrative with an increasing interest. Up to this point, no flaw in the story had turned up, but he still had a vaguely uneasy feeling.

'And then?'

'The two men came out, carrying a rolled-up rug which had something heavy in it.'

'Marcia's body?'

'Almost certainly. They heaved it into the car and rushed off in the direction of the Place Constantin-Pecqueur. I didn't have a car and couldn't follow them.'

'What did you do?'

'I stayed there, waiting.'

'Were they away for long?'

'About half an hour.'

'Did they bring the carpet back?'

'No. I never saw it again. They both went up into the flat and Jo didn't come out till an hour later.'

That held together. The two men had first taken the body to the darkest part of the Avenue Junot. As for the rug, they had probably thrown it into the Seine.

Coming back to the Square La Bruyère, they had carefully removed all trace of what had happened.

'What did you do then?'

'I waited until the next day to ring Inspector Louis.'

'Why him and not the police station, for example, or the Police Judiciaire?'

'Because that scares me.'

And he was really scared.

'It wasn't the first time you had phoned him.'

'No. I've been giving him information that way for a long time. I know him by sight. We go to the same places. He's always alone.'

'Why did you disappear?'

'Because I was afraid the Mori brothers would think of me.'

Maigret frowned. That was the least convincing part of his statement.

'Why should they have thought of you? Had you any dealings with them?'

'No. But they've seen me in bars. They know I wander all over Montmartre and that I know a lot.'

'No,' Maigret said suddenly.

The Flea looked at him with surprise, and then fear.

'What do you mean?'

'It would have needed more than that for them to decide to kill you.'

'I swear ...'

'You've never spoken to them?'

'Never. You only have to ask them.'

He was lying, and Maigret knew it, without having any proof.

'Well, we'll arrest them. While you're waiting, come with me into the office next door.

'Stay in here quietly and wait for me. Perhaps one of the inspectors has a newspaper he'll lend you.'

'I don't like reading.'

'All right. Don't worry.'

Maigret signalled to Janvier to follow him into his office.

'Did you get the Forensic Institute?'

'I got Doctor Bourdet himself on the phone. His clothes and underwear were still there. The blood is group AB.'

'The same as they found on the carpet.'

'It seems it's the most common group in the country.'

'I'm going up to see the magistrate and then I will no doubt need you and Lucas. Lapointe too.'

Maigret found himself again in the long corridor where the magistrates' offices were, where almost all the benches were occupied by people who were waiting their turn to appear. Some of them, sitting between two policemen, were handcuffed. Others were accused but still free, or witnesses, and had a less glassy look.

Maigret knocked at Judge Bouteille's door, went in and found the magistrate dictating to his clerk.

'Excuse me.'

'Sit down. It's only administrative bumf, as usual. Have you used my warrants?'

'Only the search warrant. An old Chinese rug has disappeared from the bedroom of the elder Mori brother. The carpet underneath had several spots which have been shown to be spots of blood. Group AB. Now Marcia's clothes, examined by Doctor Bourdet, have blood of the same group around the hole made by the shot.'

'That's not proof, you understand.'

'It's an indication, and there's another one. Since the evening of the funeral, Mori has slept at the Rue Ballu, and the two brothers have more or less taken over the Sardine.'

'Have you found that little midget? What's his nickname again?'

'The Flea. He's downstairs, with a good guard on him.

He confirms that a little after midnight he saw Monsieur Maurice go into the building in the Square La Bruyère where the elder Mori lives. A quarter of an hour later, Line Marcia came out and hurried home. Finally the younger Mori arrived by car, as if called in by telephone as reinforcements.

'Half an hour later, the two brothers came downstairs, carrying a heavy bundle which they dumped in the car.

'The Flea couldn't follow them to the Avenue Junot, as he had no car, but he's certain. The body was wrapped in a multicoloured carpet.'

'Do you intend to arrest them?'

'This afternoon. I would like another warrant, however, in the name of Madame Line Marcia.'

'Do you think she ... ?'

'She's certainly an accomplice. I suspect her of having handed the gun to her lover. I even wonder if it wasn't she who fired the shot.'

The magistrate turned to his clerk.

'You heard. Make out the warrant. I have an idea that they'll be hard to crack.'

'I expect so too. And it would be imprudent to send them to the assizes without solid proof, because they'll not only pay for the best lawyers in Paris, but also all the false witnesses they'll need.'

A little later Maigret went back into his office and did something he didn't usually do. He took his gun out of the drawer and put it in his pocket.

Then he called Lucas, Janvier and Lapointe.

'Come on, boys. This time we'll risk everything. You, Janvier, come with me. Go and get your gun, because we must be prepared for anything with these people.

'You two as well,' he said to Lucas and Lapointe. 'You go to the Rue du Caire. There's every chance of your finding young Mori there. If not, try his flat in the Hôtel des Iles, in the Avenue Trudaine. Finally, if he isn't there either, try the Sardine. Here's the warrant concerning him. Take a pair of handcuffs. You too, Janvier.'

They separated in the courtyard and the two cars headed towards their separate destinations.

'Where are we going?'

'To Manuel's place first.'

The concierge told them that he wasn't in, but that the cleaning-woman certainly was. They went up. The cleaning-woman was horrifyingly thin, and one wondered how she managed to stay on her feet. She was about sixty and must have been ill. The expression on her face was bitter and aggressive.

'What do you want?'

'Monsieur Manuel Mori.'

'He isn't here.'

'When did he go out?'

'I don't know.'

'He didn't sleep in his bed, did he?'

'That's none of your business.'

'Police.'

'Police or not, it doesn't concern you what bed a man sleeps in.'

'Have you noticed that the little rug that was in the bedroom has disappeared?'

'So what? If he made a hole in it with a cigarette and sent it to be repaired, that's his business.'

'Is your employer nice to you?'

'Like a prison wall.'

They were well suited to each other.

'Well, are you going to stand there? I'm going on with my vacuuming, because I haven't any time to waste.'

A few minutes later, the two men stopped in front of the house of the late Marcia.

'Is Madame Marcia upstairs?' Maigret asked the concierge.

'I don't think she has gone out. Though it's always possible to go out of the garden door, which is always open.'

'Night and day?'

'Yes.'

'So you don't know who goes in and comes out.'

'Very few tenants use that door.'

'I have the impression she wasn't alone last night.'

'I had that impression too.'

'Have you seen a man go out this morning?'

'No. He's probably still up there. According to the maid, we can expect him to be the new tenant.'

'Who was the maid more loyal to?'

'More to Monsieur Maurice.'

'Thank you.'

Maigret and Janvier went up to the first floor. Maigret rang and several minutes passed before anyone answered.

'Madame Marcia, please.'

'I don't know if she can see you. But come in.'

She had them go into the big drawing-room, which had reverted to its former appearance.

135

'We must come back here with experts on antiques,' Maigret murmured.

Instead of Line, it was Manuel Mori who appeared in the doorway.

'You again!'

'I asked to see Line Marcia.'

'She doesn't want to see you, and I'm going to stop you from bothering her.'

'I'm going to bother you both, however. In the name of the law, I arrest you.'

'Oh, the famous warrant.'

'This time there's another one, in the name of Line Marcia, née Polin.'

'You dared ...'

'I dared, and I advise you not to make any trouble. That could have serious consequences for you.'

Manuel made as if to put his hand to his pocket, where the shape of a gun could be seen. Maigret said softly:

'Put your hands down, boy.'

Line's lover was pale.

'You'd better keep him covered, Janvier.'

Maigret himself looked for a bell and he found one near the massive fireplace. He pressed it. Some minutes later, the maid stopped, disconcerted, in the doorway.

'Go and get Madame Marcia for me. Tell her to bring some clothes, underwear and toilet articles sufficient for several days.'

She came a few minutes later, her hands empty.

'What does this ...'

She stopped, seeing Janvier's gun.

'Here is a warrant in your name. I've come to arrest you both.'

'But it's nothing to do with me!'

'You were at least an accomplice in the murder, and you tried to cover up for the one who was responsible. That's called aiding and abetting.'

'If every time a woman has a lover, she risks ...'

'Not all lovers shoot the husband. Go and get some things. Just a minute. Give me your gun, Manuel.'

Manuel hesitated. His expression grew hard, and Maigret, staring him straight in the eye, prepared himself for anything.

Finally a hand held out the gun to him.

'Stay with him, Janvier. I don't like to leave the woman alone. I'm not sure that I'd find her again.'

'I have to change.'

'You won't be the first woman I've seen change. How much did you use to wear when you danced at the Tabarin?'

The atmosphere was heavy and menace hung in the air. Maigret followed Line to the end of the hall and into a pearl-grey and yellow bedroom with Louis XVI furniture. The bed was unmade. On a little table there was a bottle of whisky and two glasses, half-full.

He believed her capable of anything, even of grabbing the bottle and smashing it over his head.

He poured her a large drink of whisky and put the bottle out of her reach.

'Don't you want any?'

'No. Get yourself ready.'

'How long do you think we'll be away? Or rather, will I be away?'

'That depends.'

'On whom?'

'On you and on the magistrate.'

'What has made you decide to arrest us all of a sudden, when yesterday there was no question of it?'

'Let's say that since yesterday we have made some important discoveries.'

'You certainly haven't found the gun which killed my husband.'

'You know very well it's in the Seine, together with the blood-soaked rug.'

'What prison are you going to take us to?'

'To the *Dépot* first, in the Palais de Justice.'

'Isn't that where they put the prostitutes?'

'Sometimes.'

'And you dare ...'

Maigret pointed to the bed.

'You haven't even given this bed time to get cold.'

'You're a horrible man.'

'For the moment, yes. Hurry up.'

She deliberately stripped herself all at once, as if in defiance.

'I want to take a shower. There can't be any where I'm going.'

She had the lovely supple body of a dancer. But the superintendent wasn't at all moved.

'I'll give you five minutes.'

And he stood in the doorway of the bathroom, which had another door.

138

It took her nearly a quarter of an hour to get ready. She put on the same black coat that she had worn the previous evening, the same white hat. She had thrown a little underwear in a small case, together with some toilet articles.

'I'll go with you, since I can't do anything else. I hope you'll pay dearly for this.'

They rejoined the two men in the drawing-room. One could see from Manuel's surprised look that he had been wondering why his mistress had made them wait so long. Did he also know that she was capable of anything?

'The handcuffs, Janvier.'

'Are you going to put handcuffs on me?' asked Manuel, who had turned white and was raising his fist already.

He was much stronger than Janvier, but a long look from Maigret made him lower his fist, and the handcuffs clicked on.

'I hope you aren't going to put them on her too.'

'Only if it becomes necessary.'

The maid saw them to the door, a queer smile on her lips.

'Down you go.'

He had Mori get into the back of the car and sat there with him, while the woman sat in the front seat with Janvier. Neither of them tried to escape, which would have been futile anyway.

'What about my brother?'

'He should be at the Police Judiciaire already. Unless they've had difficulty getting hold of him.'

'Did you send your men to the Rue du Caire?'

'Yes.'

'He should have been there. My brother has nothing to do with it. I didn't even see him that night.'

'You're lying.'

'You'll have to prove the contrary.'

The car went into the courtyard and all four climbed the stairs.

'Into my office, Janvier.'

The window was still open. The storm seemed close now, and one would have sworn it was already raining in Montparnasse.

'Sit down, both of you. Janvier, see if Lucas and Lapointe are back.'

The inspector came back a moment later.

'He's next door, under strong guard.'

'Have him come in.'

Jo was as furious as his elder brother.

'I'll lay a complaint.'

'That's fine. You tell that to the magistrate.'

'How long are you going to keep us here?'

'That depends on the jury. One of you risks twenty years or more. You, you'll have a few years, anyway.'

'I haven't done anything.'

'I know you didn't fire the shot, but I also know that when your brother rang you in the middle of the night, you helped him bring Marcia's body down to your car and dump it in the Avenue Junot.'

'That's a lie.'

'Janvier! Bring in the person waiting next door.'

'If it's him ...'

'It is he, exactly. Come in, Justin. Sit down.'

Janvier remained standing, as if keeping guard, while

140

Lapointe, seated at the end of the desk, was taking the whole interrogation down in shorthand.

'Is that what you call a witness?' muttered Manuel, more snarling than ever. 'You can buy him for a hundred francs and he'll say anything you want him to.'

Maigret pretended not to have heard and turned towards Line.

'Will you tell me, Madame, if on the night of Monday-Tuesday you were in the flat of Manuel Mori, this man here, in the Square La Bruyère?'

'That's none of your business.'

'Am I to conclude from your attitude that you have decided not to answer any questions?'

'That depends on the questions.'

Her lover looked at her, frowning.

'However, you admit to being the mistress of this man?'

'I am the mistress of whom I like, and as far as I know there's no article in the Code Napoléon which forbids it.'

'Where did you sleep last night?'

'At home.'

'With whom.'

Same answer.

'Did you know that your lover had a loaded gun in or on his bedside table?'

'No comment.'

'I must insist on that question, in your own interest, because it is very important. Particularly for you.

'When your husband rang you were in bed, naked under the bedclothes. Manuel slipped on a dressing-gown to go and open the door, but he didn't pick up his gun.

141

'Your husband had a gun in his hand. He went straight to the bedroom and pulled back the sheet. What he said to you, I don't know. He turned to Manuel at once. He moved over to the bed, and a moment afterwards he had a gun in his hand. He shot first. That's the first version. In the course of the reconstruction, which will shortly take place, we'll see if it holds up.

'There is another hypothesis, just as plausible. You knew where the gun was. Your husband was about to shoot your lover and you shot first. What do you say to that?'

'I say it's pure madness. I would have had to be there first, anyway. And then ...'

Without listening to her, Maigret turned to Manuel.

'And you, what have you to say about that?'

The elder Mori looked grim and shook his head.

'I have nothing to say about it.'

'You don't challenge this theory?'

'I repeat, I have nothing to say.'

'Are you going to walk out on me like that? Well, my boy, that's not going to last long.'

'You'll note I didn't say anything.'

'You could have denied it, couldn't you?'

'I'll perhaps say something later, in front of the magistrate, with my lawyer there.'

'And meanwhile I get it in the neck. Listen, Superintendent ...'

She marched furiously towards Maigret's desk and began to speak, waving her arms about. She was no longer the elegant Line Marcia, but a wild animal broken loose.

'It's true I was in the Square La Bruyère, there's no point in denying it, because the concierge saw us, as drunk as he was, and Manuel couldn't buy him for long with a bottle of cognac. Also, my fingerprints are no doubt everywhere, and traces of powder or cream, things like that.

'For three years I've been going there at least twice a week.

'And that little guttersnipe, that midget there in the corner, must have known all about it.

'As for Manuel, he knew what he was doing, becoming my lover. It wasn't me he wanted, but to step into my husband's shoes.'

She had gone wild and was talking in a jerky way.

'When Maurice first took him on he was only a washed-up little pimp. What you don't know, I'm sure, is that Maurice was the big boss.'

Maigret smoked his pipe in little puffs and avoided interrupting the flow of words. Line was speaking in a fit of passion, or rather of fear. From time to time she turned to Manuel and looked at him with hatred.

And only a few hours ago they had been both lovers and accomplices.

Now it was a question of who would throw the responsibility on the other.

'Janvier! Take his handcuffs off.'

'At last! You've remembered. It would be difficult for me to escape from here, I suppose.'

Manuel had lost his arrogance and was merely sneering.

The Flea remained motionless on his chair, in the corner farthest away from the Mori brothers. He still looked frightened and, even though Manuel had had his teeth drawn, he still regarded him with terror.

He had been afraid of him for so long, had considered him as a kind of superman, that he could not throw off his fear.

'I'll spill the beans, as they say,' she went on. 'We were in bed. The doorbell rang.'

'You didn't expect it?'

She hesitated for a second.

'No. Why should I have expected that my husband would come that particular night?'

'He didn't know about your affair, he who knew everything that went on in Pigalle?'

'Why would he have waited three years? If he knew about it, he must have been playing a game too, for he was madly jealous.'

'Do you think that Manuel was expecting this visit?'

This time the silence was longer.

'Frankly, I don't know. He got up and slipped on the dressing-gown which was on the back of a chair. Then he got his gun out of the drawer in the bedside table and put it in his pocket.'

'She's lying, superintendent. It's a thin silk dressing-

144

gown. A gun would be seen through the material. Listen
... I said I would only talk in the presence of my lawyer.
I'm only asking you not to believe everything this woman
tells you and to check it.

'But I can tell you the truth now on one point at least.
She's the one who threw herself at me when I began to
go around with Maurice. She kept saying that he was
an old man, that he was finished. An old crank, that's
what she said.'

'No, it was he who ...'

Manuel stood up.

'Sit down.'

To an impartial observer the scene would have been
almost comical. Maigret in his chair, facing a rack of
pipes, was as expressionless as a wax figure at the Musée
Grévin. He watched them in turn, noting each one's
reactions.

The Flea was still trembling in his corner, as if danger
was threatening him personally.

The younger of the brothers was listening without
interrupting. For the moment it wasn't so much the
Marcia case which was being played out, but a bitter and
pitiless dispute between two lovers.

' "Whenever you want, you can take over from him." '

'That's what she said. She's ambitious, greedy. She
began right at the bottom of the ladder, because she did
her stint in the Place Pigalle before she worked at the
Tabarin.'

It was rather disgusting and poor Lapointe, while taking
notes, tried to hide his indignation.

'So she already had the idea of killing him?' Maigret

asked in a quiet voice, as if it was the most natural question in the world.

'At any rate, it was an idea which came to her in the first few months.'

'And you dissuaded her?'

'It's not true, superintendent. It was he who became my lover just so that he could step into my husband's shoes one day.'

'Once more, didn't he suspect anything?'

'He trusted me. Besides, it was the first time I had deceived him.'

'That's a lie. She's even slept with Freddy the bartender. He can tell you that.'

She turned to him again, full of hate, as if she was about to spit in his face.

'Things would be easier, madame, if you would sit down again.'

'I saw how you were examining the furniture and the pictures in the Rue Ballu. I'm sure you understood everything and that you're going to have them gone over by experts. They're bound to discover the secret.

'But it wasn't the idea of this shabby little man.'

So Manuel had become a shabby little man!

'The château gang, as it was called, was my husband's idea, and he's the one who organized it. There were six or seven trusted men scattered throughout France. He contacted them when an operation was planned, and they would come to the rendezvous given to them.

'The Mori brothers would be there with their lorry and some crates for camouflage.'

'What happened to the furniture and the various works

146

of art when Maurice and Manuel had had their pick?'

'They went back to the provinces, to unlicensed antique dealers. I dare you to say that isn't true.'

'That's the only true thing she's said since we've been here, superintendent. It's impossible to deny it, since the furniture will be gone over by experts.'

'But you directed the operations.'

'On the spot, yes. But the orders came from Maurice. He took no risks. In his restaurant he played the part of a reformed villain and magistrates would shake him by the hand.'

'Was it a profitable business?'

'A goldmine.'

'Which you tried to take over.'

'It was her idea.'

'Are you sure of that?'

'It's my word against hers. You can draw your own conclusions. I'm sorry I threw the gun in the Seine, for you would have found her fingerprints and not mine on it.'

'Can't you see he's lying in cold blood?'

At the moment when it was least expected, Maigret turned to the Flea, who turned pale.

'At what time did you telephone?'

'A little before midnight,' he stammered.

'What did you tell him?'

'The truth.'

'What truth?'

'That his wife and Manuel were in the flat.'

'What put that idea into your head?'

Justin turned his head away, and looked almost like a schoolboy caught out.

'Answer me.'

'I don't know ... I wanted revenge.'

'For what?'

'For everything. I tried to get into the gang two years ago. I knew how they worked. I know almost everything that goes on in Pigalle and on the Butte.

'I asked Manuel Mori to take me on and he told me he didn't need a little midget like me.'

It was Manuel's turn to speak.

'He's lying.'

Maigret smoked pipe after pipe and the air was blue with smoke.

'You may smoke too,' he said.

'What about me?' Line asked.

'You too.'

'I haven't any cigarettes, and I don't want any from that shit.'

He offered her a packet which he took out of his drawer but didn't go so far as to light the cigarette for her. Her hands were trembling so much that she had difficulty in lighting it and needed three matches.

'What's your version of the truth, Manuel?'

'He never asked me for anything and I didn't even know him, except for seeing him sometimes around the streets in Montmartre. Everyone knows he's an informer.'

'That's not true.'

'One at a time. Your turn, Justin.'

'I rang to revenge myself for this man's scorn.'

'Where did you ring from?'

'From the nearest telephone box. I could see the lights of the restaurant in the distance.'

'Did you know you were going to set a crime in motion?'

'Not absolutely.'

'But the idea didn't upset you?'

'No.'

'If it had been a question of someone else, would you have done the same thing?'

This question left him a little at a loss. He had to reflect.

'I don't know,' he confessed.

'Wasn't it your size and your face, which people laughed at, that you were getting your own back for?'

'I don't know,' he repeated.

'Pay attention to the question I am going to put to you. You have just been lying, because you are afraid of Manuel.'

149

Panic came over the midget again, as if even here the Mori brothers were all-powerful.

'I've already told the truth.'

'No. The truth is that you were paid to make that telephone call at a specific time.'

'Who would have paid me?'

'Manuel, of course.'

'I protest,' cried Manuel. 'I'd like to know why I would want to get myself caught *in flagrante* by the husband of my mistress.'

And finally Justin began to speak.

'He gave me a thousand francs. He threatened to kill me if I said anything. He added:

' "I'll have men everywhere who will do it if I can't." '

'It hurt me to do it to Monsieur Maurice, because I liked him.'

'But you did it anyway.'

'I didn't want to be shot.'

'It didn't occur to you that Monsieur Maurice might have shot first?'

'From the moment that man ...'

He pointed to Manuel.

'From the moment that man had decided how it would happen, it had to happen that way. He's a kind of devil.'

Maigret couldn't prevent himself from smiling. Line came into the foreground again.

'You see, superintendent, I wasn't lying. I didn't know about the telephone call. So I wasn't waiting for my husband to come in, and consequently I didn't have a gun ...'

'That's not true! She lies as naturally as breathing.

The phone call was her idea. I can still hear her saying to me:

' "If you kill him or have him killed anywhere, they'll get you in the end, because the police will soon find out about our relationship. But supposing he catches us *in flagrante*, as they say. I know him. He won't come unarmed. He'll threaten you. Or rather, he'll threaten me. In either case it's self-defence.'

'That doesn't prove that it wasn't you who fired the shot.'

She was crying with rage.

'But what do I have to do to make you believe me?'

'I don't have to believe you. Let me tell you again, it's the jury who will decide.'

'I've never held a gun in my life.'

'That's not true,' interrupted Manuel. 'At Bandol, I've seen her shoot seagulls.'

'With a pistol?'

'With her husband's pistol.'

'And did she hit them?'

'She killed several right in front of my eyes.'

'Justin?'

'Yes, superintendent.'

'When and where did Manuel talk to you about the phone call?'

'The night of the murder, in the Rue Pigalle. I had just taken Blanche to the Canary. I go there every night at the same time.'

'Did he tell you to ring about midnight?'

'Yes.'

'You see!' cried Line. 'I didn't even know where to

151

find the Flea, and Manuel was careful not to tell me about the phone call.'

Maigret was thirsty. He would have given a lot to have beer brought up, but he would have had to order for everybody.

He had obtained an important result, the most important. The two lovers, in attacking each other, were no longer denying the murder of Monsieur Maurice in the flat in the Square La Bruyère.

As to the guilt of one or the other, Maigret didn't attach much importance to that. It wasn't only the shot which mattered, but what had gone before, the preparation.

He turned to Manuel, who was smoking a cigarette and had an expression of defiance on his face:

'Why, since you had organized this crime of passion, did you call your brother and with him take the body to the Avenue Junot?'

'Exactly, that's proof that I didn't shoot. If I had shot him, I would have admitted it, since I would have done it in self-defence. But since it was Line, that would be more difficult to believe. I told her to go home and I promised her I would do what was necessary.'

Maigret looked at the two lovers in turn. Each one was as capable as the other of lying. Mori was a brazen character, whom nothing up till then had stopped. But was Line any more sincere than he?

A croaking voice came from the corner where the Flea was sitting.

'It was him!' the voice said.

'Did you see him?'

152

'I heard him.'

'Where were you?'

'I had followed Monsieur Maurice up to the third floor. I was hidden on the landing. At a certain moment I heard a woman's voice shouting:

'"Well, shoot then! Don't you see he's going to kill me?"

'She hadn't yet spoken the last word when there was a shot. I ran downstairs.'

There was a silence. The Flea now had a strange smile on his enormous mouth.

Manuel spoke first.

'He's lying. Maurice didn't attempt to shoot her.'

'He's making it up,' said Line. 'No one said anything.'

Maigret stood up and looked at each one in turn with a stern eye.

'Has anyone anything more to say?'

'No!' growled Manuel.

'I repeat, he's lying,' said Line.

'Janvier! Put the handcuffs on all three of them.'

'But I didn't have any part in it,' protested Jo, the younger Mori.

'Didn't you help your brother to dispose of the body?'

'That's not a crime.'

'It's called aiding and abetting. Put the handcuffs on them.'

'On me too?' yelped Line, as if she had gone into hysterics.

'You too.'

And Maigret, to Lapointe:

'Help Janvier to take them to the *Dépot*.'

153

He was tired. He wanted to think of something else. He put his hat on and went down the big staircase.

Large drops of rain were beginning to fall, which made black discs on the pavement.

He got to the Place Dauphine, where two of his colleagues were having a pastis. He was tempted for a moment, then changed his mind.

'The biggest glass of beer you have,' he said to the proprietor.

9

The bench to the left of Judge Bouteille's door was almost constantly occupied for three months. They had had to trace, in different towns in the provinces, the accomplices of the Mori brothers—and of Monsieur Maurice—in the robberies of châteaux and big houses.

Experts had laboured too and in the end had found out where the furniture and paintings in the Rue Ballu and the Square La Bruyère had come from.

Also, things stolen by the gang had been found at shady antique dealers all over the country.

Maigret had gone to Montmartre especially to congratulate the modest Inspector Louis.

'I only did my job,' he said, blushing.

'Whenever you want you can be part of my team.'

The Widower could hardly believe it. Perhaps, too, he was torn between his desire to be part of head office, so to speak, and his attachment to the Pigalle district.

The case went to the assizes in November. The case of the châteaux had been separated from it and would come up later.

In the witness-box Line and Manuel never stopped throwing the responsibility for the murder on to each other.

The telephone call to the victim implied premeditation and the maximum penalty.

155

Judge Bouteille, in spite of his patience, did not succeed in deciding between these two lovers who had become deadly enemies.

When Line was in the witness-box, one would hear a voice from the box where the accused sat.

'She's lying!'

'Be quiet.'

'I tell you she's lying!'

'And I am ordering you to be silent.'

The same scene was repeated when Manuel was being questioned.

The jury didn't settle the question. It condemned Manuel and Line to twenty years each, and Jo to five years.

And all three of them, leaving the courtroom, threw each other looks of hate.

The Flea had begun to telephone Inspector Louis again.